The Fifth Princess

Cóilín Ó Clúmháin

To Val a Friend for Many Years

Cóilín

S☼CCIONES

ISBN-13: 978-1981947423

ISBN-10: 1981947426

Design & formatting by Socciones Editoria Digitale
www.kindle-publishing-service.co.uk

Dedicated to my Mother
Eileen Clifford, who endowed me with my imagination.

Acknowledgments

Emma Sinead in Killarney, who was the inspiration for the story.

Colin, for adding words I could never think of.

Tata, for the very first edit many years ago.

Rosani and Gabriela in Brasil, for their magic.

Kenny my Irish red setter, for sitting beside me all the time.

Chapter 1

Life in Ireland in the late nineteenth to the early twentieth Century was hard; especially in rural areas, most people were living in poverty.

The young, newly ordained Father O'Daley had long wanted his Bishop's permission to emigrate. Writing many letters, he eventually received an invitation to attend a meeting at the Bishop's residence.

Father O'Daley travelled by train from his home in the village of Birdhill, near Nenagh and arrived at the Bishops residence in the late afternoon. Walking up the long tree-lined drive, he was not expecting to see such a large house surrounded by well-kept lawns and large oak trees. He approached the front door and nervously rang the doorbell. After waiting several minutes and about to ring again, a woman he presumed to be the housekeeper opened the door.

Before he could utter a word, she said, "You must be Father O'Daley, please come in," indicating with her hand to follow her. She turned and walked down a long hallway, which had many large paintings of past Bishops hanging on the wall; now and then she glanced back to make sure he was following. She knocked on the door at the end of the corridor, opened it slowly, peered in and then beckoned Father O'Daley to enter.

Expecting the meeting to be quick and to last no more than thirty minutes he entered the room but became a little nervous when he saw the Bishop with four priests sitting around a large oval table.

"Please sit down, father." The Bishop's voice was stern and unemotional as he pointed to an empty chair at the table. When Father O'Daley was seated the Bishop continued, "I have looked at your application, Father O'Daley. Why have you chosen Argentina as your destination?" Father O'Daley answered with a nervous voice explaining his request. "Argentina has a large Catholic population and I know of a small church there. It is being run by a Spanish priest, Padre Alonso, in a town called Vista Alegre Sur, and the Padre has invited me to come and work with him."

The Bishop, not showing any signs of emotion and without raising his head, peered over his glasses and asked, "Do you think that is reason enough to travel half-way round the world, Father O'Daley?"

"Your Eminence," Father O'Daley replied, "It is difficult for me to explain. I strongly feel it is my destiny and in the fulfilling of that destiny, I will be doing what God has chosen for me; Ireland is well catered for with priests, and I look forward to the challenge of spreading God's word to the people of Argentina and Patagonia."

The meeting lasted around one hour. Finally, the Bishop suggested Father O'Daley wait outside while he discussed his application with the four priests.

After a short time, which seemed like hours, the Bishop asked Father O'Daley to return to the meeting. He sat in the same seat and feeling apprehensive, placed his two hands on the table.

The Bishop, looking down at the papers on the table spoke without raising his head. "Father O'Daley, we have considered your application and have decided to grant your request. Let me be the first to congratulate you and give you the full blessing and support of the church. Father Morrissey," pointing to the priest on his right, "has agreed to help you arrange your trip." The Bishop stood up and held Father O'Daley's hand tightly. "I wish you a safe passage and a successful parish."

With the blessing of his Bishop and a little help from God, the young Father O'Daley began his journey. On the Tenth of August 1930, he made his way from Dublin to Queenstown (now known as Cobh) in the county of Cork, where his journey to Argentina was to begin. Boarding the ship at Queenstown, he was soon heading across the Atlantic on his way to New York on the first leg of his journey. Father Morrissey had arranged lodgings for the young priest at a local Catholic church near the docks.

After several days rest, Father O'Daley continued his journey and boarded the passenger ship Trancarville. Steaming through the South Atlantic with several stops in Brazil, the ship eventually docked at Buenos Aries. After resting for a few days in a local Catholic church he continued the arduous journey south, to the small town of Vista Alegre Sur in Patagonia. There he joined the small Catholic church established by the

Spanish priest Padre Christano Alonso. Both Padre Alonso and Father O'Daley worked well together, and with much help from the small local community, Father O'Daley was almost fluent in Spanish after the first year.

Just before Easter, during his second year in the parish, Father O'Daley was busy draping dark purple silks over the statues in the church; a ritual always observed at this time of the year. Padre Alonso approached him. "I would like to have a word with you when you have the time."

"I have time now", answered Father O'Daley, as he climbed down the small ladder. Both priests sat down facing the Altar. Padre Alonso was the first to speak, explaining that he was leaving to go and visit the little church attached to the university hospital in Buenos Aries, but first he would make a trip to the small town near Lago Pellegrini where he had served in his first parish.

A little surprised, Father O'Daley asked, "Will you be going to another parish?"

"I have a mission Father O'Daley; to save the lives of children not yet conceived."

"I will pray for you and your mission," Father O'Daley whispered. "When do you leave our parish?"

"Soon after Easter, it will give me a little time to say goodbye to the parishioners."

Padre Alonso left the parish two weeks after Easter. Three weeks later,

Father O'Daley received a phone call from the police station at Lago Pellegrini asking if he knew where Padre Alonso was, as his car had been found abandoned near the lake. Father O'Daley explained why the Padre had gone there; the police informed him that Padre Alonso had not arrived at the church. Days became weeks then months: They never found Padre Alonso, it was presumed that he had drowned. The locals had reported a large Aurora Australis over the lake two days before the car had been discovered. The older inhabitants of the village insisted he was carried away by the angels to work with God.

The local people rallied round Father O'Daley. He became more involved in the local community, and he would never look back. He wrote many letters home to his Bishop, explaining the rich opportunities available in his parish for hard-working Irish boys. After many months of waiting, he received a reply from his Bishop. "There is one young man I know," the Bishop wrote, "has the spirit of adventure, he lives with his parents on a tied farm, in the village of Ballycommon near Nenagh."

With Father O'Daley's powers of persuasion, the Bishop organised the payment for the young Thomas O'Houlihan to travel to Argentina. After a few years of working on local small farms, Thomas had saved enough money to buy, under a special Government scheme, a large piece of good farmland of almost 3000 acres.

Thomas O'Houlihan was a true Celt who kept to his religious faith. Every Sunday he would travel the 5 miles to Father O'Daley's church. Never wanting to forget that it was with Father O'Daley's and Gods help that he was here.

Thomas wrote many letters home, but as time went by, the return letters got fewer and fewer; the last letter he received was from his mother to tell him that his father had died. The letter read as follows:

Son, I write to you today to tell you your father died a few weeks ago. He had a long illness, and God decided it was his time. Son, with the help of our neighbours we gave him a lovely funeral. He is now resting without any more pain at Holy Cross Abbey, where he always wanted to be.

I suppose by now you have a girlfriend. Well! You tell her I said she's got a fine lad; you know son, I am not much for this writing business. God Bless, Your mam.

Thomas wrote many more letters home but never got a reply.

A few months later at a Sunday service Father O'Daley called Thomas into the sacristy and gave him the news. "Thomas!" he said in a soft voice, "I have just had some news from Ireland. Your dear mother passed away in her sleep a few weeks ago. They say she missed your father too much, she is now resting alongside your father, Jack, at Holy Cross Abbey."

"You know father, they worked so hard on that useless piece of land, they never had anything," said Thomas.

"Thomas!" Father O'Daley said in a loud voice, "they brought you into this world and look at you now, a successful farmer; this was the job God had chosen for them."

"I wonder what God has for me?" Thomas asked.

Father O'Daley looked at him and smiled. "I am sure he is already working on The Plan." "Thomas, I will put a notice in the church letting everyone know; we will hold a special service for your mother and father next Sunday."

"Thank you, Father," answered Thomas.

The following Sunday everyone from the village came to the church service.

To the surprise of Thomas all the parishioners came and consoled him. He knew then that he had made the right choice in coming to Argentina.

Father O'Daley approached him. "Thomas there is someone I would like you to meet." Then turning round he said, "Thomas, let me introduce you. This is Garcia Ramirez and his wife, Teresa. Garcia is now our new mayor; their beautiful daughter Isabel is over there by the Altar."

Teresa called her daughter to come over. "This lovely lady is Isabel," Father O'Daley said smiling.

"Isabel comes here every Tuesday at midday with fresh flowers for the Altar."

As Thomas shook her hand, Father O'Daley could almost hear the wedding bells; he knew then this was part of God's plan. This was going to be a match made in heaven.

On the Tuesday of the following week, Thomas unexpectedly arrived at the church. Father O'Daley looked up, "Is it Sunday already?" he joked.

"Father, I was just passing and thought I would come in and say a little prayer," blurted Thomas.

"She usually comes in with fresh flowers around midday," answered Father O'Daley.

"Oh, is that so," said Thomas, trying to look anywhere but at Father O'Daley.

Before Father O'Daley could speak, the church door opened, and who should appear but Isabel. In Spanish, she said, "Father I am so sorry I thought you were alone." Father O'Daley just smiled, he could see the surprised look on her face and the glint in her eye. "Please come in, Isabel." And with a soft Spanish accent she said, "Mr O'Houlihan it is so good to see you again."

Father O'Daley decided to leave the rest of the work to God and made an excuse to leave.

Over the next few months, Thomas and Isabel would see much of each other. Love blossomed quickly. They married early the following year, and soon had their first child, a girl christened Anabella, and two years later, a boy.

The years went by quickly. Anabella, now 18 years old, left the farm, and entered university, eventually marrying a lawyer. They moved to the city of Mendoza, had one child, a girl christened Ellinor.

When Ellinor was born, her health took a turn for the worse and she nearly died. Her mother, Anabella, always said she survived because she was special.

Thomas never saw his grandchildren; he died in a farming accident. Isabel remained on the farm with her now married son; she passed away five years later. Both Isabel and Thomas are now resting in peace on a hill looking down on the farm. Father O'Daley lived to the ripe old age of 85 years and passed away peacefully in his sleep.

At Ellinor's thirteenth birthday, Anabella gave her a little ornate box and explained, "Many years ago after your grandfather died, Father O'Daley gave me this little box."

Ellinor opened the box, she could see some old photographs, a folded card and a tooth wrapped in piece of cotton. Anabella explained, "The photographs are of Father O'Daley and your grandfather." Ellinor opened the card carefully, she could see there was a lock of hair. "Is that grandad's hair?" she enquired. "Yes, it is," her mother replied. "Father O'Daley cut your grandfather's hair the first day he arrived and kept this lock. I am not sure why Father O'Daley put a tooth in the box, but I do believe it was your grandfather's. He asked if one day I could return it to your grandfather's place of birth in Ireland." Anabella continued, "Perhaps one day in the future Ellinor, you can make this trip." Ellinor answered, "I will keep this safe mother, and maybe one day in the future I will get the opportunity to take it to grandfather's home."

"He was a great man, Ellinor," Anabella said. "He was brave to leave his family and home so far away and begin a new life here. He and Isabel, your grandmother, loved each other very much." Ellinor could sense sadness in her mother's voice. Throwing her arms round her mother, she said, "Mama, one day together, we will take great-grandfather's spirit to his home in Ireland."

After several years, Ellinor moved to Buenos Aires studying Modern Educational Methods at the Universidad de Buenos Aires. It was there she met the young trainee doctor, Jose de Salvador. They married in 1994 and lived in a modest size house in the suburbs of Buenos Aries.

Chapter 2

April 2, 1998, 06:00: Buenos Aires University Hospital, Mrs Ellinor de Salvador gave birth to her first child, a girl. The birth was premature, being almost a month before her full term.

Her husband doctor, Jose de Salvador, a Surgeon at the Mari De Santos Hospital, three Kilometres from the University Hospital, drove through the city traffic to be with his wife. He arrived just as the nurse was placing the child in an incubator in the next ward. As he greeted his wife and sat on the bed alongside her, he asked, "Where's our daughter?" Tears streaming down her face, she replied in a low voice, "she's not well." The Midwife interrupted, "As the baby is premature, we have moved her to intensive care as a precaution. Everything will be fine," she assured them.

"I understand," replied Jose.

Over the next two days, everything was well. Ellinor now back home and visiting her daughter daily, spending many hours sitting by the incubator holding her daughter's tiny hand.

On Saturday the 4th of April, on his return from his work at the hospital, Jose asked his wife, "How is our daughter today?" "My God, she is so tiny," she replied. "I feel we should have her christened soon, especially as her health is not good. I will speak with Padre Matthew about it tomorrow."

"Sounds sensible to me," Jose replied.

Ellinor spoke the next day with Padre Matthew after the Sunday service. He is the Padre of the small church attached to the hospital. The christening would take place on the afternoon of Thursday 9th of April, in the children's emergency ward. Only four guests would attend. Jose, and his brother Henriki, Ellinor and her mother Anabella.

Early morning of the 9th, the family arrived on the ward. Padre

Matthew and two of the ward sisters were already there. Ellinor and her family stood close to the incubator. Padre Matthew reached into the incubator and gently dampened the little girls head with holy water and spoke: "As the Almighty God is our witness I christen you Emma Sinead de Salvador."

Ellinor held her husband's hand and said in a gentle voice, "You have a name. Miss Emma Sinead de Salvador, you have a name."

After the ceremony, they walked to a small waiting room just outside the ward. Padre Matthew spoke softly, "Mrs de Salvador, I am curious why you chose the name Emma Sinead."

Ellinor paused for a moment, "It was a suggestion from mother," she said looking towards her mother. Her mother Anabella continued, "Padre Matthew, when I was a young child my father Thomas O'Houlihan used to tell me stories about Ireland. Tales of leprechauns and fairies living in his garden."

"But of course," Padre Matthew replied, "your father was from Ireland."

"Yes he was," Anabella answered, and then continued. "One day, father said to me, when you grow up, marry and have children you must name the girl Emma Sinead." I said, "Father, I may not have a daughter, and why that name?"

He answered, "My child, you *will* have a daughter, and it's a name fit for a Princess. When Ellinor was christened, I did not have the opportunity to name her Emma Sinead, as both my husband and his family insisted on the name Ellinor."

Padre Matthew answered, "With those two beautiful names Emma Sinead, will grow up to be beautiful, gracious, and of course clever." Anabella said, "She will grow up to be a Princess just as her great-grandfather told me."

Over the following few days, Ellinor never missed her daily visit to the hospital. One day while sitting by the incubator, a monk walked into the ward and introduced himself.

"My name is Padre Christano Alonso." Ellinor looked at him and reached out to shake his hand; as he softly held her hand, she commented, "I've not seen you here before Padre."

He hesitated before answering, "I was the Padre in a little church in the State of Patagonia. Many years ago, the Bishop of Buenos Aries selected me to be the Padre of this hospital church, but God had a different plan for me."

"Where is your church now?" Ellinor asked, "Mrs de Salvador, my church is everywhere I go."

"She is beautiful, don't you think?" said Ellinor as she looked towards her daughter. "Yes she is," remarked the Padre "and tiny. I understand she has been christened by padre Matthew?"

Ellinor smiled and answered, "Yes, just a few days ago, and her name is Emma Sinead de Salvador." "That's a lovely and fitting name for a girl." "Thank you," replied Ellinor as she stroked the baby's hand

"Mrs de Salvador, I must beg forgiveness," the Padre said as he slowly got to his feet, "I have a busy schedule and must bid you farewell." He tenderly held Ellinor's hand and in a soft voice said, "Do not worry, I know she will be fine." As he left the room, he hesitated for a moment and said, "Emma Sinead is a *very* special child."

"I know," Ellinor replied, "I know."

Chapter 3

On Good Friday, while in his office at the Mari De Santos hospital, Doctor Jose received an urgent call from the University Hospital. "Doctor de Salvador, this is Doctor de Lima from the University Hospital." "Good morning Doctor de Lima, how can I help you?" he replied. "Doctor de Salvador, I think it would be advisable for you to get to the hospital immediately. Your daughter's condition is worsening." As the doctor hurried out of the hospital he telephoned his wife, directing her to go to the hospital and where to meet him.

Both parents entered the Emergency Ward at the same time. Two nurses were connecting monitoring equipment to the baby. Jose and Ellinor could see and hear the heart monitor, the green line jumping and a fast beep, beep, beep sound. Doctor de Lima approached, "I am sorry," he said. "Your daughter is having difficulties with her breathing and her heart rate is fast." He continued, "We are doing everything we can to stabilise her."

"She was doing well," Ellinor said in a soft voice, "what caused this?"

"I am not sure at the moment, but I suspect an infection. We need to do some tests immediately," Doctor de Lima answered.

Ellinor, holding her husband's hand, was at last able to see her daughter, wires and tubes were covering all the little child's body. She glanced up at the small picture of the Virgin Mary hanging on the wall and muttered softly, "Please, I don't want to lose her." Jose felt helpless; because of the ethics of his profession, he could not intervene or offer any advice.

Suddenly, without warning, the heart monitor gave a long continuous sound. Doctor de Lima immediately started to massage the baby's chest. The monitor continued to make a noise. Turning to a nurse, he said in a calm voice, "Oxygen Now!"

Jose looked at his wife, "Let's wait in the other room."

"No!" she said, "I'm not leaving her." With tears now streaming down her face, she rested her head on her husband's shoulder. After what seemed like hours, but in fact was only minutes, Doctor de Lima turned to Jose and Ellinor. "I am sorry, we have done everything possible. There is nothing more we can do." Ellinor gripped her husband's coat tightly as she buried her head in his shoulder. Now facing the door, afraid to turn round and look at her daughter's lifeless body, she saw through tear filled eyes, the figure of Padre Alonso standing and smiling; indicating to her to hold her daughters hand.

Ellinor released her grip on her husband and walked towards her daughter, who was now lying still as if sleeping. Holding her hand out she stroked her daughter's arm. Jose reached out as if to hold her back, Dr De Lima held his arm and quietly said, "Leave her, she has to do this."

Ellinor ran her finger down the full length of the baby's arm and called her name, "Emma Sinead, Emma Sinead, it's Mama." Then reaching the little girl's hand, placed her finger in the palm of her daughter's hand, and in a low voice said, "Please come back. Don't leave me now."

Just at that moment, with such a drama taking place, no one noticed the florescent tubes in the ward turn from white to a pale green. And, as if her daughter had heard her mother calling, immediately four tiny fingers squeezed tight on her mother's finger. The heart monitor gave one little bleep then another and another. Within the space of a few seconds, Emma Sinead de Salvador had returned.

Dr. de Lima was almost speechless, "I don't understand," he said. While he was talking, Emma Sinead's colour returned, and her breathing was back to normal. Dr. de Lima spoke, "I need to do some testing, to find out why this happened and to prevent it happening again."

Ellinor looked at her husband and said in her soft voice, "It won't happen again, she is special."

Holding Ellinor's hand tight, Jose spoke, "They need to do the tests my dear, let's wait outside."

Ellinor repeated, "I know it won't happen again."

"Let's pray everything continues as it is now," replied her husband. "We are all thankful to God for his intervention."

"I would like to go to the church to thank God and the Padre for their intervention," Ellinor said.

"Let's walk there now," answered her husband, "Emma Sinead will be fine. Someone up there is looking after her." Ellinor looked up to the picture of the Virgin Mary and said, "Yes, they are."

Jose and his wife made their way down the long, winding passageway towards the little church. After several minutes they arrived at the door. Jose reached out and pressed at the heavy wooden door, the hinges creaked as it opened. They stepped inside and immediately noticed the strong, distinctive smell of old wood and incense. The church was small, with only ten rows of wooden seats lining either side of the aisle. The twelve stations of the cross positioned on the walls and in preparation for Easter, each statue covered with a purple shroud. Jose and Ellinor walked slowly down the aisle, trying not to make any noise, but every step reverberated on the stained wooden floor. Approaching the altar, they noticed a lone figure kneeling in prayer.

Ellinor spoke in a low voice, "Padre Alonso." The Padre turned round, a confused look on his face. "Mrs de Salvador," Padre Matthew said, but before he could continue, Ellinor spoke, "I am so sorry, I thought you were Padre Alonso.

We came here to thank God and the Padre for his intervention."

Reaching out, and holding the hands of both Jose and Ellinor, Padre Matthew said, "I have just heard the good news! Sometimes God works in mysterious ways and look at the time it is 15:00 hrs, the time when Jesus ascended into heaven." Then, looking to Ellinor, Padre Matthew asked, "Mrs de Salvador, why were you expecting Padre Alonso? He is no longer with us, it's been about sixty years."

Not thinking of how many years had passed she asked, "Which Parish is he now in?" Now more confused than ever, Padre Matthew hesitantly answered, "I do believe Padre Alonso had an accident and was presumed drowned in a lake, near his parish in Patagonia, I think about sixty years ago."

"It's not possible, I don't understand," replied Ellinor. "I met him twice, and he looked no more than twenty-five years old. He introduced himself and clearly said his name was Padre Christano Alonso. Speaking in a hushed voice she said, "Two weeks ago, while sitting with Emma Sinead, a monk came into the ward. He introduced himself as Padre Christano Alonso." She continued, "Today I saw him at the door of the Emergency Ward. He smiled at me and indicated for me to hold Emma Sinead's hand. But when I looked again he was gone."

Padre Matthew interrupted, "Mrs de Salvador, I do recall the Bishop telling me, when I came here to take over this little parish, that a Padre Alonso drowned in a lake while visiting a church near a small town in Patagonia, just a few days before he was due to take over this church. Please let me look into this a little further, and talk with the Bishop. Meanwhile let us say a prayer, thanking God and Padre Alonso for their intervention." All three knelt at the Altar, Padre Matthew reciting a prayer of thanks. Ellinor looked up at the purple clad statue on the Altar, smiled and softly said, "Thank you."

Just when they were about to leave the church Padre Matthew said, "Please wait a moment, there is something I wish you to see." He rushed out, and returned carrying a paper folder. "Mrs De Salvador," Padre Matthew said, as he opened the folder and handed an old photograph to her, "do you recognise anyone in this photo? It shows a group of people at a Church conference here in Buenos Aires many years ago."

Ellinor de Salvador looked at the photo and immediately pointed to a cleric standing in the middle of the group. "That's who I saw," she said, pointing to a figure in the photograph. "Is that Padre Alonso?" she asked.

Padre Matthew took the photo in his hand. "You are right, Mrs de Salvador, it is Padre Christano Alonso. Please, I beg of you, let me investigate this further. I will contact the Bishop, he may throw some light on the mystery."

Padre Matthew took their hands, "I promise as soon as I have any news I will contact you both. Meanwhile, you have a daughter to visit."

Shortly after making sure their daughter was ok, they both left the hospital and walked out into the street. Ellinor looked to her husband, "Jose, listen to the birds! Even they have heard the good news!"

Over the next few weeks, Ellinor visited her daughter every day. She spent many hours just holding her hand and remembering the words of Padre Alonso.

After some weeks of monitoring Emma Sinead, Dr De Lima agreed she could now go home. Jose and Ellinor de Salvador walked out into the warm, May sunshine carrying little Emma Sinead de Salvador. The young Princess was going home.

Chapter 4

12 years later

Buenos Aires: August, four thirty in the afternoon. Twelve-year-old Emma Sinead de Salvador has just returned from school. "Mama," she calls out, "In our history lesson today, we learnt all about London. The teacher played a short film about the Queen's Palace, a big clock they call Big Ben and Westminster Abbey. Mama, I would love to go there one day, maybe even meet the Queen." Her mother just smiled and said, "I am sure one day your dream will come true. Whether or not you also meet the Queen, I do not know. I can just imagine the guard at the Palace: Excuse me Ma'm, Miss Emma Sinead de Salvador from Buenos Aires is here to see you." Ellinor laughed, "Somehow my dear, I cannot see that happening."

Emma Sinead answered, "Mama, maybe one day it will happen and I will ring you from the Palace."

"OK Miss Dreamer," her mother said, "sit and have your lunch before your father comes home."

Emma Sinead's parents were both professionals. Her mother an adviser to the Educational Department of the Government, her father, a surgeon at the local hospital and her grandmother Anabella Fernandez, a retired diplomat and civil servant.

While eating her lunch, Emma Sinead was all chatter about her school and her friends. "Mama" she called out, "I would love to use the internet, I could look up many interesting places in London for when we go there." Her mother looked at her with a serious expression on her face. "First you must ask your father about the Internet, and second when are you planning our trip to London?"

Just then the door opened and Dr Jose came in, "My God, it's getting cooler out there," he said. Before he could remove his coat: "Papa! Papa!"

Emma Sinead blurted, "Mama said one day, we are going to go to London."

"Emma Sinead, I do not remember saying anything like that," interrupted her mother.

"Well, I suppose I had better leave my coat on then, if we are going to London," her father replied smiling. "Are we leaving now?"

"Papa I'm serious," answered Emma Sinead, "and Mama said you would let me go on the Internet."

"Emma Sinead!" Ellinor said in a raised voice, "I suggested you should discuss the Internet with your father, but not now as he has had a busy day and needs a rest." Her father quickly took charge of the conversation. "First, I will take off my coat, then I will eat, relax a little and read my mail, then I am free to discuss the London trip and the Internet."

Emma Sinead continued the chatter, her father cut her short by placing his finger to his lips; she knew this was not the time. Silence reigned at the dinner table.

Dinner over, Emma Sinead had gone to her room and began to practice on her Pan Pipes. The haunting sound weaved its way through the house. Jose, downstairs checking his mail, and peering over the top of his glasses. He commented, "She's getting good on Pan Pipes, that's a beautiful tune she's playing."

Ellinor answered from the kitchen, "I don't know what music it is, she just started playing that tune last week."

"A beautiful piece of music, a haunting sound." Jose replied.

"Her music teacher is surprised at her ability to pick up music so quickly," said Ellinor, "she has the ability to listen and play. In fact, all her teachers are delighted with her progress, especially in mathematics and the sciences. By the way, do you think she is old enough to go on the Internet alone?"

Jose looked up, "I think she is a responsible young girl, I have no objection, providing she does not let her education suffer."

"Very good," Ellinor answered, "I will set up the laptop in her room. Do we need to get someone in to connect her computer?" she asked.

Jose, reading one of his letters, looked up and said softly, "Yes, ring the repair man, I am sure he can do it." He continued, "I had a letter today from the Medical Association inviting me to lead a group of doctors to a medical conference in the United Kingdom, the end of March, in the city of Brighton at the University."

"What a coincidence, Emma Sinead was just talking about going to London. That is the beginning of spring in England," Ellinor answered.

"Well, if it is anything like this country, it could be winter. Remember my dear, summer starts in Europe around mid-June," he answered. "I would hate to be going earlier and have to wear my winter clothes!" he laughed.

Ellinor smiled and said, "We could all go to the United Kingdom. What a lovely birthday present for Emma Sinead." She continued, "It's hard to believe that almost thirteen years have passed so quickly."

"Look at her now," Jose replied, "12 years old and as tall as a house! Let me get more information about the conference, and possible dates. Yes, I suppose we could all have a holiday and a birthday present for Emma Sinead." He continued, "Let's not say anything to her at the moment. Otherwise we will never have any peace!"

Emma Sinead came bounding down the stairs and burst into the room. "Did I hear someone talking about the United Kingdom?" she asked.

"Your ears are too big for your head, Emma Sinead!" her father blurted out as he put his letters in his briefcase, then he looked up and said "and one step at a time on those stairs."

"Sorry Papa," Emma Sinead answered.

Her mother quickly changed the conversation. "Your father has agreed, you may go on the Internet." Emma Sinead almost jumped on her father, "Thank you, Papa, I promise I will only use it for my studies and talking to my friends."

"But please remember what your father said, it must not interfere with your studies." Emma hugged her father, "Thank you, Papa."

"OK," her father said. "It's late and past your bedtime." Emma Sinead went to her mother and kissed her, "You're the greatest parents," she said. "I cannot wait to tell my friends in school tomorrow."

"Papa, Mama, I love you both the same," she said as she climbed the stairs. "Well I am glad we don't have to compete for your love and affection," her mother said as she laughed.

"Now let me see what is happening in the World," Jose said as he switched on the TV to the evening news.

17

Chapter 5

The months went by quickly. Now, the day before Christmas Eve, plans were in place for the grand Christmas party. Both Emma Sinead and her mother were preparing the food. Emma Sinead spoke, "I hope Grandmama comes early." Just then, Anabella telephoned to say she was almost at the house.

Ellinor called out, "Emma Sinead! Your Grandmother is on her way." Just as she spoke the doorbell rang.

"It's Grandmama!" Emma Sinead shouted, as she ran and opened the door. She threw her arms round her grandmother and gave her a big hug.

"My God you have grown so much," her grandmother said. "Let me look at you." Emma Sinead took a step back. "To think you were once only this size," pointing to her little finger.

"Grandmama, I was never that small!" laughed Emma Sinead.

Ellinor came rushing out, still with her apron on, and gave her mother a big hug. "I hope you had a good journey," she said. "I know the trains are always busy at this time of the year. Emma Sinead! are you going to let your Grandmama stand there holding those heavy bags, or will you invite her in?"

Emma Sinead answered, "Sorry Mama! Grandmama, I will take your bags to your room, you go and sit with Mama."

As they walked to the other room, Anabella remarked, "You are so lucky, Ellinor. Emma Sinead is turning out to be a well-mannered and beautiful young lady."

"Mother," Ellinor replied, "we are so grateful to you for all your support in the early years, and of course to the good Lord for blessing our family."

"What time will Jose be home?" Anabella asked.

"He telephoned me earlier to say he would try to be home by three thirty, he mentioned that he had some good news."

Emma Sinead came bounding down the stairs. "Grandmama! We are all going to a special church tonight. And on Christmas eve night, we are going to the Cathedral, so we are free all Christmas day."

"Sounds like a big party is in the wind."

"Oh yes, Grandmama!" Emma Sinead said, "Papa has invited some friends for Christmas dinner and my friend Maria is coming with her parents."

"Well! In that case, I had better put on my party hat and clothes," Anabella answered.

Jose arrived home from the hospital a little later than he had planned.

"Are we ready for church?" he asked.

"Yes," replied Ellinor, "just waiting for mother to come down."

"Anabella, it is so good to see you," said Jose as he gave her a kiss on the cheek.

"What about me?" asked Emma Sinead. Her father put his arm round her shoulder, "All the hugs and kisses in the world for my Princess."

While driving away from their house Jose said, "Tonight, we are going to a special church." Ellinor just smiled. When the car drove into the University Hospital, Emma Sinead asked, "Papa are you going to visit Padre Matthew?"

"Yes, Emma Sinead," he replied. They parked the car and entered the university hospital. They walked down the long corridor towards the little chapel. Ellinor, squeezing her husband's hand spoke in a low voice, "Every time I come here I feel so calm and peaceful." "It's where it all began," he replied. When they reached the door of the church, Padre Matthew was standing there to greet them. "Anabella, I am so glad you could make it here for Christmas, and you, Emma Sinead de Salvador, it is a pleasure to welcome you to my little church."

"Thank you, Padre," Emma Sinead said. Walking with them into the church they made their way down the aisle and sat in the front row.

"The service will begin in about 15 minutes," Padre Matthew said and walked away. Ellinor knelt in prayer and looking at the altar, she remembered that day almost 13 years ago and thought about Padre Alonso. She turned to Jose and quietly said, "I must ask Padre Matthew did he ever find out any more information about Padre Alonso." The little church filled very quickly, mostly with past patients of the hospital. The service began with a mass and after it had ended Padre Matthew gave a short sermon and wished everyone a very happy Christmas. As the Salvador family left the church they reminded Padre Matthew of the Christmas party.

Christmas Day in the Salvador house, now buzzing with excitement, all the guests have arrived. "Where is Emma Sinead?" asked Anabella.

"I think you will find her in her room with her friend Maria," Ellinor replied.

"I expect she is on the internet talking to school friends."

"Well in that case, I will leave her," replied Anabella.

Padre Matthew walked over to Ellinor. "It has taken a long, long time, but now I have some information about Padre Alonso. I have to apologize, I am afraid the wheels in the Vatican move very slowly."

"I was about to ask you had you heard anything," answered Ellinor.

Padre Matthew spoke, "Ellinor, I have not come with all the answers, but we have some information. I do believe the Bishop contacted many parishes in different countries."

He opened the letter sent to him by the Bishop, and began to read: "Dear Padre Matthew, I know we have spoken many times over the past few years about Padre Alonso, but as you know the wheels of the Vatican move very slowly. After requesting a search in the Vatican archives for references to the late Padre Alonso, and in parishes overseas, we at long last have had some success. They found the following information, but please remember we have no way of verifying any of the claims made at the time. A young mother in the Ukraine, formally part of the Soviet Union, claimed a Priest visited her and saved the life of her new-born girl. She said the Priest called himself Padre Alonso. The second case was in Sorrento, Italy 1992, a third in Spain 1994 and finally, another in Tokyo, Japan in 1996." Padre Matthew looked at Ellinor and continued reading aloud. "All the claims made were well documented in their local parishes, and are similar to your case. But we have no way of following up these claims as it's been a long time and families and priests have moved. Finally, as all the records describe similar events they will need more investigation. In the meantime, please give my best wishes to the Salvador family." The Bishop of Buenos.

Ellinor was silent for a moment and holding her mother's arm spoke, "I do not understand, do you think it was Padre Alonso?"

"I don't know, Ellinor," Padre Matthew replied. "I do know from reading about Padre Alonso, he came from a large family of true Celts, originating from Galicia Spain. He was very passionate about peace in the world and had a great love for children. I have taken a copy of the letter and this original is for you." He folded the letter carefully and placed it in her hand.

"It seems we have more questions than answers," Ellinor replied.

"It does seem so," answered Padre Matthew and added, "If true, then your daughter Emma Sinead has a good angel on her shoulder. She will always be in safe hands." Through all this conversation, Anabella remained quiet and as Padre Matthew walked away, she turned to her daughter, held her hand and said, "One day I know you will get all the answers."

Ellinor replied, "I hope so mother, I would dearly love to meet Padre Alonso again and introduce him to the child, or should I say young lady he saved all those years ago."

"If you truly believe, then it will come about," Anabella answered.

Just then, Emma Sinead appeared with her friend Maria, and in an excited voice said, "Mama! The Internet is great. We have talked with all our school friends and we could see them."

Ellinor smiled, "Modern technology is taking over the world," she said. "But I wish it were all for the better."

Anabella spoke, "Well young lady, in my day, if we had a telephone in our house, we were very rich."

Suddenly the voice of Jose was heard. "Please everyone gather round, a special toast to all our friends, my work colleagues and especially to our dearest friend Padre Matthew. Not forgetting my lovely wife, my mother-in-law Anabella and of course my beautiful daughter Emma Sinead." He continued, "We have all had a wonderful year, and may our good fortune continue well into the next."

Chapter 6

The party ended in the late afternoon and all the guests had left, except for Maria. Ellinor suggested they retire to the lounge for a quiet family get together.

"Papa, you said you have great news for us?" Emma Sinead asked.

"Yes I do, but it's not that exciting," her father replied as he glanced over to his wife and winked his eye. "Earlier this year, I received an invitation to lead a team of doctors to a medical conference, which is to take place in the city of Brighton in England, near the end of March next year. Your mother and I will be going to the United Kingdom on the 24th of March."

Emma Sinead was almost speechless, "Papa what about me?"

"You young lady, will be staying with your grandmother. It's only for one month, and we will ring you every day." Emma Sinead was devastated. "Papa, it will be my birthday!" Emma Sinead's face dropped. The disappointed look was more than Ellinor could bear. She reached out and held Emma Sinead's hand. As she did so, the lights in the house dimmed and for a moment turned a pale green. "It must be a power surge," Jose commented.

Ellinor continued, "Emma Sinead, do you think for one minute we could travel the world and leave you here? Of course you are coming with us! You are going to celebrate your birthday in the United Kingdom! Your father is only joking."

"Grandmama," Emma Sinead asked, "is this true? Are we going to England? Are you coming with us, Grandmama?"

Her grandmother replied, "Yes, you are going to England, but unfortunately I cannot travel with you. There is so much I have to do."

Ellinor spoke, "Your grandmother has a busy schedule here in Buenos

Aries and cannot travel with us, but she will live here in our house until we return, and you can call her every day if you wish."

Jose spoke, "Emma Sinead, the look on your face when you thought you were not going with us was priceless."

"Papa, that was most unfair of you," answered Emma Sinead.

Jose continued, "Your mother will inform your school of our impending trip on your return after the Christmas break."

"Mama, can I go on the internet and tell all my friends," Emma Sinead blurted out.

"Not so fast young lady, don't you think you should sit for a while and talk to your grandmother?" said her father. "That's fine," answered Anabella, "let her go and tell her friends. After all, you do not get news like that every day." The excited voices of Emma Sinead and Maria could be heard as they rushed up the stairs.

Ellinor gave the letter she received from Padre Matthew to Jose, and after reading it carefully, he commented. "This is very strange indeed, but I am sure there is no connection, maybe just a coincidence."

Anabella said quietly, "Perhaps Padre Matthew will get some more information, or it may remain a mystery forever."

"Intriguing," replied Dr Jose.

Later Jose, Ellinor and Anabella were relaxing in the lounge. The haunting sound of panpipes could be heard throughout. Anabella put her finger to her lips, but said nothing. After a few moments, Ellinor looked at her mother and noticed a tear running down her cheek from the corner of her eye. "Are you alright mother?" she asked.

"It's that music," she replied. "It brings back so many memories of my childhood."

"Emma Sinead has been playing that tune every day for the past three weeks," Jose said, "I think it's in her music book."

Anabella spoke softly, "You know that was the song your grandfather would sing to me when I was a child, he had a lovely voice." Just then, the music stopped and Emma Sinead came bounding down the stairs and into the room.

"My friend Maria is on the internet talking to her brother," she said.

"Emma Sinead, where did you learn that beautiful tune you were playing?" her grandmother enquired.

"I don't know Grandmama, it was just some music in my head," she replied.

"Is it music from one of your books?" asked Eleanor.

"No Mama," Emma Sinead answered. I have no idea where I heard it."

"Would you play it for me?" asked her grandmother.

"It's not perfect yet, Grandmama, and I do not know it all," Emma Sinead answered, "but I will play it for you." She went quickly to her room and was back in the lounge in seconds holding the panpipes. She stood in front of everyone and began to play. As she played, her grandmother began humming the tune. A tear slowly ran down her cheek and at the same time a smile was on her face.

Emma Sinead stopped playing and spoke, "Grandmama, that is all I know." Anabella looked to her granddaughter, "Emma Sinead you played that beautifully."

"Grandmama, you know this music?" Emma Sinead asked with an enquiring voice.

"Many years ago, when I was your age, your great-grandfather used to sing that song. It's called Boolavogue. I believe the song was composed by a man from Ireland. Your great-grandfather was a great man for storytelling about life in Ireland, and his favourite story was of naughty fairies swimming across from Scotland to steal his chickens, and can you imagine I believed it."

With an enquiring look on her face Emma Sinead asked, "Grandmama did fairies really steal great-grandad's chickens?"

"Your great-grandfather had a vivid imagination! But who knows, maybe they did steal his chickens, and while he was working he was always humming that tune."

"Grandmama," Emma Sinead asked. "How do you think I know this tune?"

"Maybe you heard me humming it one time," Anabella replied.

"Emma Sinead," her mother spoke, "It's time for bed. You have had a long day."

"Mama, can Maria share my room tonight?" Emma Sinead asked.

"Let me telephone Maria's mother first, before you two make plans." Ellinor walked into the kitchen and returned moments later, "OK," she said, "Maria can stay, and we will drop her off tomorrow, but no talking all night please."

"We will only talk for a short time, Mama," Emma Sinead answered. Giving each a hug and a kiss, Emma Sinead was on her way to bed.

Anabella spoke, "Ellinor, we are all so fortunate to have a young lady like that in our lives."

"I thank Padre Alonso for his intervention when we needed him most and I thank God for blessing our family." Just as Anabella and Ellinor walked from the lounge to the kitchen, Emma Sinead now in her room, called out, "Grandmama, will you come and talk with me for a short time?"

"Of course, just as soon as I have helped your mother in the kitchen," she replied. "Mother you go and talk with Emma Sinead, Jose and I will sort the kitchen out." Anabella walked into Emma Sinead's room. Maria was fast asleep on one bed. Anabella sat on the bed next to Emma Sinead. "Well young lady, what shall we talk about?"

"Grandmama, I have something to ask you."

"Oh dear, this sounds very serious," Anabella said.

"No, it's nothing serious Grandmama, I want to ask you about a dream I had."

"Ok, let's hear about your dream," her grandmother answered.

Emma Sinead started her story, "Two nights ago, I had a dream. There were four beautiful girls."

"Perhaps they were your imaginary friends," offered Anabella.

"Grandmama! I am nearly thirteen. I don't have imaginary friends any more. Grandmama, the girls I dreamt about were talking in different languages and they all understood each other."

"I think it was all the excitement of Christmas." Anabella knew what was happening and replied not wanting to frighten her granddaughter, "Sometimes, if you have had a hectic day, you dream more, sometimes dreams do come true. Perhaps one day, you will meet these beautiful girls and you can tell them, I met you in my dreams."

"I hope so," Emma Sinead responded. "They were so beautiful."

Now, Emma Sinead!" Her grandmother said, "Off to sleep and have many more sweet dreams."

A little later, while sitting in the kitchen with Jose and Anabella, Ellinor spoke, "Something strange happened this evening, and I do not understand why. Remember when I touched Emma Sinead's hand and the lights faded and briefly turned green? At that moment, I felt such a great surge of happiness, it is difficult for me to describe: Like a force emanating from Emma Sinead."

"You are probably overtired my dear," replied Jose. Anabella said nothing just smiled. "I think you are right answered Ellinor, let's all retire for the night."

Next morning the Salvador family set off early to visit friends and deliver the Christmas presents. Taking Maria home first, the trip round Buenos Aries to visit friends took them most of the day, returning home in late afternoon. Once inside their home, Jose smiled and said, "I love to visit people, but it's always nice to come home."

A day later, Ellinor and Anabella were in the kitchen preparing a light snack. Emma Sinead was sitting at the table in the lounge with a sheet of plain white paper and a pencil. "Are you writing your holiday list already?" her father asked. "No Papa, I am drawing a picture of some girls for Grandmama."

Later, Emma Sinead handed her grandmother a sheet of paper. "What's this, a present for me?" her grandmother asked.

"It's the sketch of the four girls in my dream," Emma Sinead replied.

Ellinor spoke, "Are these your imaginary friends?"

"Mama, these are my real friends."

Ellinor looked to Anabella and smiled. Anabella opened the piece of paper,

"What a beautiful drawing" she said, "are you learning art in school?"

"No Grandmama," Emma Sinead replied, "I just know how to do it. Grandmama! Do you think I will meet these girls one day?"

"Only the Good Lord knows that answer my dear, may I keep this drawing?" her grandmother asked.

"Grandmama, it's my gift to you." Folding the piece of paper carefully, Anabella said, "I will keep this in a safe place, and one day, if I meet these girls, I can show them the sketch and tell them you met them in your dreams."

Later in the evening Ellinor spoke to Anabella. "Sometimes I worry about Emma Sinead and her imaginary friends."

Anabella replied, "Ellinor, Emma Sinead inherited the gift of imagination from her great-grandfather. I am sure one day in the future she *will* meet these girls."

"Mother," Ellinor said, "is that normal for a twelve-year-old?"

"Ellinor, it is normal for Emma Sinead, I can feel my father's presence when she is beside me. I am sure he is by her side and guiding and protecting her. After all, to him, she is a Princess."

A few weeks later while finalising his plans for the conference in the United Kingdom Jose realized he needed hotel accommodation for six doctors and their wives, and his family of three. Searching through the internet for accommodation in Brighton, he could see that one hotel was close to the conference centre; The Belmont Hotel. Jose sent them an email, and after around thirty minutes came the reply. They could only take three people, but would be prepared to get accommodation for the other five doctors and their wives nearby. The doctor decided to take the offer and sent back a reply, giving them a full list of names and informing them that he, his wife, and daughter would be staying in the Belmont Hotel. Three days later, he received confirmation of the booking, stating they would be in contact two to three weeks before the conference was due to start.

Chapter 7

Alex Andrusanko, owner of the Belmont hotel, contacted his friend Patrick Ahern, the new owner of Bunratty castle hotel near Limerick in Ireland. Patrick is also president of the Irish Celtic association.

"Patrick, I have some news for you and also I need your help. Over the past few months rumours have been spreading though out the Celtic organization pertaining to the arrival and Crowning of the fifth Celtic Princess. I am now convinced that she has arrived, or at least will arrive shortly at our hotel in Brighton." Alex went into all the details regarding the medical conference and the de Salvador family coming to the UK from Buenos Aries.

"Patrick! My daughter Nikita saw the girl's name on the booking register a few weeks ago and immediately said that she is the fifth princess. Now before you ask, yes Nikita is very sure this is the girl we have been waiting for."

"Ok Alex, what would you like me to do?" asked Patrick.

"I need you to trace the girls ancestry and find out if there is a Celtic connection."

"Alex, it's strange you should ask for that information, I have a colleague in the Irish Embassy in Buenos Aries and he has just finished compiling a list of all Irish immigrants to Argentina since the early nineteen hundreds. I will send him an email as soon as we are finished talking."

Two weeks later Alex had just finished lunch. The receptionist informed him a Mr Patrick Ahern was on the phone.

"Good afternoon my Irish friend," Alex said in a loud booming voice.

Patrick laughed, "Sorry Alex, did I wake you up?"

Alex laughed and responded, "You would have to wake up very early, Patrick, to catch me in bed."

"Alex, I have some interesting news for you about Irish immigrants to Argentina. In the early nineteen hundreds, a young boy left a village called Ballycommon, just five miles from the town of Nenagh and travelled to Argentina. His passage was organized by the church, and his name was Thomas O'Houlihan. We know he married and had a daughter named Anabella. We also know she married a lawyer, I believe called Fernandaz. She is now a retired very respected diplomat."

"That's amazing," replied Alex. "I've just purchased a hotel in Ballycommon! Patrick, I have many friends in government here. I am sure one of them will know of an Anabella Fernandaz. I'll be over there next week with Nadia, can you book us in for two nights next Thursday and Friday?"

"I would be delighted to," answered Patrick. "Any change of plans, let me know."

"Thank you, Patrick, talk to you soon."

Immediately Alex put the phone down, he dialled the Foreign Office in London and asked to speak with Michael Hagen.

"May I ask who is calling sir," the receptionist asked.

"Can you tell Mr Hagen it's Alex Andrusanke."

After a few moments Michael answered, "Alex! What can I do for you?"

"Michael, I was wondering if you had ever come across the name Anabella Fernandaz in your records."

"Just a moment, let me check," answered Michael. A few moments later, he came back. "Alex, I need to know why you are looking for information on Mrs Fernandez and it's spelt with an e not an a."

Alex started to explain what was happening.

"Stop! Michael said loudly, I urgently need to come and talk with you." Michael said, "You have the right lady, but we cannot discuss it further on the phone. Alex, I can drive down to Brighton tomorrow. I think it's important that we meet quickly."

"Ok Michael, I'll see you for lunch around midday. Can I inform Nadia?"

"Yes, that will be fine. See you at lunch time tomorrow."

After Alex put the phone down, he walked quickly to the penthouse.

"You look confused," Nadia said as he entered the apartment.

Alex replied, "More than you can imagine." He explained everything.

Nadia responded, "My dear, you're not listening to the news! Something is brewing between the UK Government and Argentina, and you seem to have hit a nerve."

"Well! Well!" said Alex. "We will know tomorrow. Michael Hagen is coming to lunch. When I mentioned Anabella Fernandez to him, he shut up like a clam and refused to discuss it any further on the phone."

Midday, the following day and Michael Hagen arrived at reception. The receptionist escorted him to the penthouse.

"Michael, it is so good to see you!" said Nadia, "Alex is on his way, please sit down." She pointed to the sofa overlooking Brighton Promenade. "Would you like something to drink before lunch?"

"Thank you, Nadia, coffee would be fine. I think this time, Alex hit the jackpot with the Foreign Office. Every alarm bell was ringing. We thought we had a spy!"

Alex arrived and as they sat down to lunch. Michael explained that Mrs Anabella Fernandez was a retired senior official in the Argentine Government and was very highly thought of, both in Argentina and in the UK. "I had the pleasure of meeting with her several times, both before and after the Falkland Crisis. She's a lovely lady and a true diplomat."

"Alex and Nadia, what I am about to tell you cannot be repeated to anyone outside this room." Michael went on to explain that negotiations were due to take place between the two governments regarding the Falklands, or as they say in Argentina, the Islas Malvinas. Both Governments agreed that a different approach was necessary.

"One idea that is looking very likely, and a precursor to amicable negotiations, a young Argentinean would be presented to a member of The Royal Family. This meeting would be broadcast on international television stations worldwide. Mrs Anabella Fernandez suggested her granddaughter would be the perfect choice."

"This information was passed to our Ambassador in Buenos Aries, and the wheels were set in motion. A member of the Argentinean Foreign Office has spoken with Mrs Fernandez and has met and approved the young girl in question, even though neither the girl nor her parents were aware of his identity and they are totally ignorant of our strategy. That's why it must remain secret until we have finalised our plans. This event

30

would be scheduled to take place in mid-April and we are just waiting for confirmation of dates."

He then produced a photograph of the young girl and passed it to Nadia. Nadia looked at the photo and sat silently for a moment. "I cannot believe this," she muttered.

"Does it mean something to you Nadia?" Michael asked.

Nadia stood up and walked quickly to the lounge, returning with a folded paper in her hand and spoke, "Michael, before I show you this, I want you to know there is more going on than you can ever imagine. Last week my daughter Nikita told me she had a dream. In that dream she saw a young girl holding her hands out and calling her name. This is the drawing of the girl Nikita drew just two days ago." Nadia handed the drawing to Michael. He looked at it, and placed the drawing on the table beside the photograph of Anabella and her granddaughter. Michael looked bemused. "I am totally mystified, it's the same girl."

Michael then explained to Nadia and Alex, Anabella had faxed him a sketch her granddaughter had drawn of four girls she had seen in a dream. The young girl told her grandmother there were four girls, all speaking different languages. She gave the sketch to Anabella as a gift.

Michael placed a photograph of that drawing on the table. Nadia looked and said, "Michael, I hope you are prepared for this, please go in the lounge and look at the photograph of Nikita and her three friends that is on the table." Michael returned with the photograph in his hand. "Do you recognise any of them?" Nadia asked.

Michael looked incredulous. "This is uncanny!" He said as he compared the drawing to the photograph. "She has never seen these girls or a photograph?" he asked.

"Never!" Nadia replied.

Michael answered, "This is so strange, the detail in this drawing is unbelievable! Are these girls here in England?"

"No," replied Nadia. "All are different nationalities, just like the young girl told her grandmother. One lives in Italy, one in Spain and one from Japan and of course Nikita lives here."

Alex looked towards Michael, "The connection to all of this, we believe, is Celtic: Each of the girls is of Celtic origin."

"But both of you are Russian," replied Michael. "And where is the

Celtic connection to your daughter."

"My grandfather was Irish and fought in the Russian revolution, and later he changed his name to Andrusanke." Alex continued, "Michael, the next part is going to be more difficult for you to comprehend." Alex then explained as well as he could, the history of the four girls and the possible connection to Miss Emma Sinead de Salvador.

"How do you know her full name?" demanded Michael, "I've not mentioned it!"

"Michael, did you know she'll be staying here?"

"You mean in this hotel?" asked Michael.

"Correct!" replied Alex. He produced the list for the medical conference. An Argentinean; Doctor Jose de Salvador is leading the conference.

"There's her name," pointing to the list. "Emma Sinead de Salvador and her mother, Ellinor de Salvador."

"This is crazy," said Michael, staring at the photographs on the table. "How can I talk about this? People would think I had gone mad."

"Michael, you asked us not to mention the Argentine talks or the meeting with a member of the Royal Family. Now I ask you not to mention what I have just told you. But when the family arrive here, I will call you and you may come down and observe the girl. In fact, you can meet all the girls. They will also be here." "This is unbelievable!" remarked Michael. "At least now we know she will be in safe hands while she is here."

"Very safe, I can assure you," replied Alex.

Michael left the hotel to return to London, promising to keep Alex informed as the situation progressed.

Chapter 8

Alex and Nadia arrived at Shannon airport in his private jet. Patrick Ahern was waiting outside to meet them and after clearing passport control, they drove the fifteen kilometres to Bunratty Castle Hotel. Alex and Nadia checked in to the hotel and agreed to meet with Patrick later for dinner.

During dinner, Alex was the first to speak. "Patrick, we are now sure this young girl will be the fifth princess."

"You must have discovered more information!" answered Patrick.

Nadia took the drawings and photographs from her bag. She placed them on the table and pointing to a drawing she said, "This was drawn by the young girl from a dream she had, now look at this photograph of our four girls."

"My God!" said Patrick, "It's like looking at two photographs, the drawing is perfect, and it's just like our girls."

Nadia spoke, "Alex told you of the dream that Nikita had a few weeks ago.

Patrick this is Nikita's sketch of the girl in her dream." Then handing Patrick a photograph, "This is a photograph of the young girl and her grandmother taken 4 weeks ago."

Alex interrupted, "Patrick there is a definite connection between this girl," pointing at the photograph, "and our four girls."

"Alex," Patrick asked, "you said she is coming over to the United Kingdom in April, who has organised that trip?"

"It seems that her father, a surgeon, is leading a group of doctors to a medical conference in Brighton and that's all I know." Alex said.

Nadia butted in, "Patrick, there are things happening, involving the British and Argentine Government's and this girl is playing a small part, but due to security we cannot tell you anything right now."

Patrick spoke with a confident voice, "Alex I think you are right, The Celtic Gods are at work. We must be patient and let them complete the task." He continued, "Do we know if this girl or her parents are aware of the situation?"

"We don't know," answered Alex, "but we will be very cautious when she arrives, and leave it to The Gods and their endeavours."

After dinner, when Patrick had left, Alex and Nadia spent the evening relaxing and discussing their plans for the following day. An early breakfast next morning, they drove in Patrick's car to the Forge Hotel in Ballycommon to inspect the renovations, spending almost all of the day there. They returned to Brighton later the following day.

Chapter 9

Christmas was a distant memory in the Salvador household, only three weeks to go before the journey to the United Kingdom. Jose was finalising his plans, not only for his trip, but also for replacement doctors to stand in for the ones going to the United Kingdom.

On returning to his home, the sunlight was already fading. Jose opened his front door and Emma Sinead rushed down the stairs to greet him.

"Papa, I am all packed and ready to go!" she said.

"Emma Sinead," he replied as he hugged her, "you were all packed last month, last week and now today! Will you be packing again tomorrow?"

As he made his way into the lounge he said, "Emma Sinead, twenty kilos only. We do not want the contents of your room!"

"I know Papa," she replied. "Papa, do I have to go to school during the last week?" she asked.

Her father answered, "I think you should finish your school the Friday before, and on the Monday both of us can go to collect your grandmother and bring her to Buenos Aires. By the way Emma Sinead, where is your mother?" "Mama went to the supermarket. She wanted to stock up the freezer with meals for Grandmama," she replied.

Jose turned on his laptop and checked his mail. There was one new mail in the inbox from the Belmont Hotel, confirming his reservation for Friday 26th of March to the sixth of May. It read as follows:

Dear Dr. de Salvador,

May I take the opportunity to confirm your reservation at the Belmont Hotel for you, your wife and daughter, beginning on Friday 26th March to the 6th of May? You enquired about the distance from the University conference centre. I enclose a map which should give you all the information you need. Could you please forward your flight details by a return email. I will arrange for a member of my staff to meet you and your family from either Gatwick or Heathrow Airport. I hope you and your family have a pleasant flight.

Sincerely, Alex Andrusanke.

One hour later his wife had returned. "My dear," Jose spoke, but before he could continue, his wife replied, "I do need to put all this frozen food in the freezer for mother, before I sit down and talk with you." She then called out "Emma Sinead, can you please come and help me?"

"Yes Mama," as she came bounding down the stairs.

Jose spoke in a loud voice, "Emma Sinead! Please be careful on those stairs!"

Her mother joined in, "Emma Sinead! The stairs have steps and you come down one step at a time, not five!"

"Sorry Mama," she replied.

"Let's have dinner first." Jose said "We are then free for the rest of the evening to discuss our plans."

During dinner, Emma Sinead informed her father she was going to re-pack her luggage. "Good!" her father joked, "there will be room for your mother's clothes as well!"

"Papa," she replied, "It's harder for a lady to pack. We have to worry about things like fashion and colour, and of course, we have to look our best. Just wait until Mama starts packing!"

"Very well young lady, you win," her father replied.

After dinner, all three sat down and went over their plans for visiting the United Kingdom. Emma Sinead spoke, "Mama, Papa, I wrote out a list of all the places I want to see in London, and some other cities. Can we go to Stonehenge?"

Jose took the list from her hand and with his eyes raised to heaven, he said,

"Young lady, we are going for just over four weeks, not four years!"

"I can make a list a little shorter," she responded.

"Emma Sinead, if you remove twenty items from the list, it will still be too long."

"Papa," she exclaimed, "all my friends in school have added places of interest for me to visit."

"Emma Sinead, please inform your friends that they can see all these places on the internet. Now off you go and re-pack while I talk with your mother."

Jose gave a copy of the email and the downloaded brochure to his wife. She carefully read the email and then spoke as she looked at the brochure. "It sounds and looks like a very nice hotel. I see from the map, the conference centre is almost next door." Jose replied, "After I received the email I telephoned the hotel today, and spoke with the owner. He and his wife are Russian. He also told me his daughter is a lecturer in the University." Ellinor interrupted, "Remember the letter my dear, that Padre Matthew gave us. One girl was Russian."

"I'm sure that is just a coincidence," Jose answered. "There are plenty of Russian people in the world!"

The following day, Ellinor sat down with Emma Sinead. She spoke in a low voice, "I have a little box your grandmother gave me many years ago. It contains a photograph and a lock of hair and tooth from your great-grandfather." She continued, "A long time ago, it was given to your grandmother by a Padre O'Daley, who was from Ireland. He asked if it could be returned one day to where your great grandad was born." As she handed the little box to Emma Sinead, she said, "The United Kingdom is not far from Ireland, maybe an opportunity will present itself and we can complete the task."

"Mama," Emma Sinead replied, as she peeked inside the box, "I will treasure this with my life. I'm sure we will complete the task." Ellinor gave her daughter a hug. As she stood up, she was sure for a moment the lights turned to green, she felt a great calmness come over her: The same feeling she had the day she walked out of the hospital, so many years ago with her newly born daughter in her arms, and also remembering the evening at Christmas when she held Emma Sinead's hand. Somehow, she knew everything would be alright.

Chapter 10

Jose received a reply from the United Kingdom Visa section, requesting he attend a meeting at the Embassy on Tuesday morning at eleven thirty.

Driving to the appointment, Emma Sinead was chattering as usual, "Papa, maybe the Queen will be there to greet us."

"You, young lady, have a very active imagination!" her father replied. He continued, "Somehow, I cannot see the Queen of England being there to greet the Salvador family." Parking their car, they walked to the entrance of the building, and going through a strict security check, they were shown into a large room. Emma Sinead was the first to point to the large portrait on the wall of Queen Elizabeth. "She looks like a real Queen," she said.

Just as Ellinor was about to answer, the door opened and a man dressed in a pinstriped suit came in. He introduced himself as Head of visa control. He asked a few basic questions about the medical conference and turning to Emma Sinead asked her, what places she would like to visit. Jose interrupted him and laughed, "I'm afraid sir she has a list so long we would need to be here for at least a year."

The meeting lasted around thirty minutes. The official spoke, "Doctor de Salvador, I hope you and your family have a pleasant holiday in the United Kingdom," and handed him an envelope. "Your visas and all your documents, Doctor de Salvador and if I may comment, your choice of hotel in Brighton was the correct one. I have stayed in that hotel many times, it's highly recommended."

A few days later, while in his office at the hospital, Jose received a call from the British Embassy. "Doctor Jose de Salvador?" the voice said.

"Yes, this is Doctor de Salvador."

"Doctor, my name is Karen Knight and I am the secretary to the United Kingdom's Ambassador, Mr John Bloomfield."

The doctor answered with an enquiring voice, "Is there a problem with our visas?"

"No doctor, it's nothing to do with your visas," she replied, "the Ambassador has asked me to contact you. He would like to have a meeting with you within the next few days. About a different matter, but relating to your planned trip and it's best not discussed on the telephone. Would next Friday at ten thirty be OK for you to come to the Embassy?"

"Just a moment," Jose answered, I will check my diary." After a brief silence, he spoke. "Yes, that would be fine, I am free all day."

"Doctor, I am sorry for such short notice, it was completely unavoidable."

"Can you tell me anything about this meeting?" he asked.

"I can only tell you doctor, it has to be kept completely confidential and you may be pleasantly surprised." She continued, "As you are free all day Friday, doctor, let me organise lunch with the Ambassador."

"Thank you very much," he replied, "I will be there at ten thirty this coming Friday."

That evening in the Salvador house, after Emma Sinead had gone to bed, Jose called to his wife, "Remember, we are going shopping on Friday."

"Dear, you are not working again, you need a day off," his wife answered from the kitchen.

Jose asked her to come into the lounge. "Please sit down," he said pointing to the sofa. "I hope this is not bad news?" she asked as she sat down.

Jose spoke in a soft voice, "The British Ambassador has requested a meeting with me this coming Friday."

Ellinor spoke, "Surely that is very unusual. We are only going for a conference and a holiday, or maybe it is something to do with your conference?"

He replied, "It's strange because the meeting must be kept completely confidential. And I was also told that I might be pleasantly surprised."

"Why secrecy?" his wife asked. "It must be something important."

"Maybe they want to recruit me as a spy," Jose said laughing.

"Something is going on," his wife said, "I read the other day that talks may begin soon to resolve the Malvinas issue."

"Well let's wait and see what Friday brings."

On Friday morning, Dr Jose arrived at the Embassy at exactly 10:30. He had learnt that punctuality was a British trait. When he reached the entrance, the porter asked, "Are you Doctor Jose de Salvador?"

"Yes," the doctor replied, as he handed his identity card to the porter.

"Please follow me sir," the porter said, as he walked towards the door leading to the Ambassador's private residence. The porter knocked on a closed door before entering. Jose followed behind, and as he entered the room, Karen Knight, the secretary to the Ambassador greeted him. She spoke as she held out her hand, "Doctor de Salvador, I am delighted to meet you."

"Please take a seat, doctor, I will inform the Ambassador of your arrival."

After a short wait, the Ambassador entered. "Doctor de Salvador! I am so glad you could come at such short notice." Shaking his hand, he then indicated for the doctor to follow him. They entered a medium sized lounge, the walls decorated with photographs of the Royal Family. Both then sat on a large sofa.

"Doctor de Salvador, would you like coffee?" Karen asked.

"Yes please, no sugar," he answered.

When Karen had left the room, the Ambassador spoke. "Doctor de Salvador,

I am sure you are aware of the talks that may take place soon between our two governments."

"Yes, very vaguely," Jose replied.

The Ambassador continued, "As a precursor to talks, and to smooth any tensions, both the United Kingdom and Argentinean Governments are exploring the possibility of a young non-political person to be presented to a member of the British Royal Family. doctor, I will get straight to the point. My Government and your Government would like your daughter, Emma Sinead, to be presented to a member of the Royal Family in the United Kingdom."

Jose sat in stunned silence for a moment, and then he spoke, "Am I hearing this correctly Ambassador? You would like my daughter to meet with a member of the British Royal Family?"

The Ambassador smiled and looked straight at the Jose. "That is correct doctor. Now, let us have lunch and I will explain as much as I can to you. Please remember, no word of this meeting to anyone outside this room, but of course, you may discuss it with your wife."

Dr Jose left the Ambassador's residence at four thirty in the afternoon. His head in a spin from the news he had just received. On entering his home he was surprised not to see Emma Sinead.

"Is our lovely daughter upstairs packing again?" he enquired.

"As it's Friday, I let her stay in Maria's house," Ellinor answered. "We can collect her tomorrow. Well? Do not keep me in suspense! What was the meeting about?"

Jose looked at her, smiled and said, "I think you had best sit down."

Ellinor sat on the sofa and with a puzzled look on her face said, "From the smile on your face, this is something good."

He began, "Cast your mind back to Christmas, when Emma Sinead was talking about all the things she would do when in England."

"Yes, I still have the list she wrote," Ellinor answered.

"Ellinor, not the list, something she said."

"Oh yes, I remember," said Ellinor, "she said she might have tea with the Queen."

The doctor looked at his wife. "Ellinor, our daughter Emma Sinead, may not be having tea with the Queen, but will be visiting the Palace as an Ambassador for our country."

Ellinor sat in silence for a moment, then asked, "Is this really true, or are you joking?"

"It is true," Jose said. "Ellinor, no one outside this room can know anything about this, not even Emma Sinead. We can only tell her when we are given permission."

"Why pick our daughter?" Ellinor asked.

"My dear, I don't know why she was selected. But I do know the suggestion emanated from here in Buenos Aries and was confirmed by the Government in the United Kingdom."

"It's going to be difficult to keep this secret from her," Ellinor said.

Jose replied, "We must not give her any idea that something like this is going to happen..."

"Can we at least tell my mother?" Ellinor asked.

"Yes, we can," replied the Jose. "But do not telephone her. Let's wait until we meet."

"Jose, with all that excitement, I forgot to tell you that mother has purchased a large house just outside the city."

Jose replied, "Emma Sinead is going to be very happy with that information!"

Ellinor answered, "Mother and I decided not to tell Emma Sinead until we go to see the house. We can say we are going to meet with some friends."

"Sounds like a good surprise!" answered the doctor.

Two days later, the Salvador family were on their way to see Anabella's new home. Emma Sinead had no idea where they were going or who they were going to meet. As they drove up the long tree lined driveway, she commented to her mother, "Mama, what a lovely place to live! It is so peaceful."

"It is a beautiful place, my dear," her mother answered, "perhaps one day, we will have a place like this."

"Papa, the people that live here, are they friends of yours?" Emma Sinead asked.

"Yes, I suppose you could call them friends," he said smiling.

As they got closer to the house, Emma Sinead noticed a woman standing outside. "Mama, look, that lady looks like Grandmama." Then she shouted, "Papa! It's Grandmama!"

After all the hugs and kisses, they went inside. "Grandmama!" Emma Sinead, blurted out, "Is this your house?"

"Yes it is, my child," she replied, "I just wanted to be closer to you and of course, to my daughter and her lovely husband."

While Emma Sinead and her mother were out exploring the grounds. Jose took the opportunity to tell Anabella the news regarding the visit to the Embassy. He was a little surprised by her lack of excitement. He looked at her and said, "You already know?"

"Yes, I know all about it," was her reply. Anabella explained, she had a phone call with a friend of hers who was high up in Government. He had told her it was very likely that Emma Sinead would be meeting the Queen and Prince Phillip. They were waiting for more information from the British Government.

"Well, Anabella," Jose replied, "It's nice to have spies in the right places!"

She laughed, "It does help from time to time." A few moments later, Ellinor and Emma Sinead returned. "Papa," Emma Sinead said, "there is a big lake and another big house further down the road."

"They are my neighbours," replied Anabella.

Chapter 11

On Thursday 25th of March, the Salvador family boarded their flight to London, changing planes at El Dorado airport in Colombia which meant a wait of several hours. Emma Sinead loved every minute as she sat in the transit lounge at El Dorado airport. The long wait did nothing to dampen her spirits; fascinated by hundreds of people milling round. This was the beginning of a great adventure for her.

After round two hours, they heard the announcement, "Will passengers for flight Avience 121 for London, please make their way to Gate twelve, the flight is now boarding." They made their way there and quickly boarded the plane. They settled in for their ten hour flight to the United Kingdom. With a time difference of plus six hours, they would arrive around one o'clock in the afternoon.

Their uneventful flight landed on time and the Salvador family quickly made their way through winding corridors towards immigration control, where they joined the long queues of people who had arrived from other flights. After around ten minutes and with no movement of the queue, Jose remarked, "This could take us hours." Just then an official came walking through the crowds calling the name of Doctor Jose de Salvador and family.

"I am Doctor de Salvador," Jose answered. "May I see your documents Sir?" The official asked. Jose opened his carry bag and handed the three passports to the official. After checking all three passports he said, "Thank you, doctor, could you please follow me." They walked through a side door into a small room. "Please take a seat," he said, as he pointed to three easy chairs, "I hope you and your family had a pleasant flight, especially you, Miss Emma Sinead. Was this the first time on a plane?" he asked.

"Yes," Emma Sinead replied, blushing a little as she spoke in English.

He then handed the documents back to the Jose. "Doctor de Salvador, on behalf of the British government, we welcome you and your family to the United Kingdom." He continued, "I believe you are being met by Miss Carolyn White from the Belmont Hotel."

"That is correct," he replied. "One of my colleagues will escort you and your family through to the baggage hall and take you through customs."

Jose thanked him, and after a short wait in the baggage hall, they walked straight through to customs and out the door into the meeting area. Jose commented to his wife, "We have just had the royal treatment!"

He was surprised by the number of people milling around and worried that he may not be able to see the representative of the Belmont Hotel, when suddenly Emma Sinead spoke, "Papa look there, over there!" she pointed across the hall.

"There, by the information desk." Jose looked over and spotted the woman with a placard with his name printed on it. They walked over to where she was standing.

"Excuse me," Jose spoke, "are you Miss Caroline White?"

"Yes I am," she replied, "and you must be Doctor de Salvador and family." Jose introduced his family. "This is my wife, Ellinor, and my daughter Emma Sinead."

"Bienvenido a Londres Doctor de Salvador y una gran bienvenida a youe esposa e hija. Mi nombre es Caroline Blanco, seré tu conductor para la duración de su estancia en el Hotel Belmount."

"Miss Caroline," Jose smiled and replied in English, "your Spanish is perfect, but we intend to live like the famous proverb, when in Rome do as the Romans do."

Caroline replied, "I am delighted you speak English! You will enjoy your stay here much more. Please let me organise your luggage." She then hailed a porter. On leaving the airport, Caroline told them that the journey should take no more than 1hour 30 minutes.

"Mama," whispered Emma Sinead, "look, the steering wheel is on the wrong side." Ellinor answered, "The British do everything differently my dear."

Caroline laughed, "All the people from the Americas comment on the steering wheel."

Arriving at the Belmont Hotel, Caroline drove into the underground car park. She called the porter on the intercom to come and collect the luggage, and then walked with the Salvador family to the lift and reception area. After they exited the lift, they walked towards the reception desk and Caroline introduced them to the receptionist. She continued, "If you and your wife or, of course, Emma Sinead need to go anywhere, I am at your disposal 24/7, just ask reception. It's all part of the Hotel courtesy service."

As she turned to leave, Isaac, the Irish Red Setter, owned by Nikita Andrusanke, the daughter of Alex and Nadia Andrusanke, peered out from behind the reception area desk and was quickly noticed by Emma Sinead. "Mama look," she said in Spanish. Her mother reminded her to speak English. "But Mama, look" she said in English pointing to the reception desk. "Look at the dog! Mama he is very cute."

"Be careful my dear," replied her mother. "He may be a guard dog."

The receptionist laughed, "Isaac, a guard dog? He's afraid of a mouse! He's a very inquisitive dog, and likes to meet everyone that comes into the Hotel."

"Is that his real name?" Emma Sinead asked, "and can I stroke him?" Before anyone could answer, Isaac was by her side, his tail wagging like a propeller.

"Well, Miss Emma Sinead," the receptionist said, "it looks like you've made a friend for life."

"I hope so," was her reply, "he is beautiful."

While Jose stood at reception filling out the registration forms, Emma Sinead and her mother walked over to the easy chairs and sat down. Isaac followed and sat beside Emma Sinead.

"Emma Sinead," said her mother, "you have a new friend."

"He is so cute Mama," replied Emma Sinead.

As she stood up and walked round, Isaac followed, and when she stopped, he stopped.

"Mama," she said, "Isaac is so funny. He just follows me everywhere I go!"

Jose called to his wife and Emma Sinead. The porter had already placed their luggage in the lift. As they walked over to the lift, the receptionist called to Isaac, "Isaac! you are not allowed in the lift! Come back here and wait for Miss Nikita."

Reluctantly, Isaac sauntered over to the reception area, glancing back at the lift as the doors closed. When they entered the penthouse, the porter walked over and opened the curtains to reveal a large panoramic view, looking straight down at Brighton beach and promenade. "This is beautiful!" exclaimed Jose. "I did not expect this."

The porter asked, "Sir, if your daughter has an IPad, she can connect to our free internet service. The password is IsaacAndrusanke."

"Thank you," replied Ellinor as the porter left.

Ellinor turned to her husband, "I hope they have not made a mistake with our accommodation."

"I hope not," replied Jose. "The penthouse must be expensive."

"It must be a mistake," replied Ellinor. "I will check again with reception," and picked up the phone.

"Good afternoon, can I help you?" the voice said. "I'm sorry to bother you," replied Ellinor, "I was just wondering, are we in the correct room?"

"Oh yes Mrs de Salvador," replied the receptionist. "It was Mr Andrusanke's instructions that you stay in the penthouse suite and of course, at no extra cost to yourselves."

"The accommodation is beautiful, more than we expected," Ellinor replied. "We hope you like it Mrs de Salvador, the kitchen has been stocked with food for your use, but none of it is Argentine i'm afraid. Is there anything you need Mrs de Salvador?"

"No, we need nothing at the moment, thank you very much." Ellinor replaced the phone. Turning to Jose, "It's not a mistake my dear, and at no extra cost."

"Mama," said Emma Sinead. "Can I use my Ipad?"

"Of course," she replied. "Can you remember the password?"

"That's easy," replied Emma Sinead. "There are two names, IsaacAndrusanke."

Within a few minutes, Emma Sinead was talking with her friend Maria in Buenos Aries.

Chapter 12

After the conference had ended, Alex Andrusanke instructed Caroline to organise the three-day visit to London for the Salvador family. They left the Belmont hotel early to avoid the London bound traffic. On arrival, Jose and Ellinor were surprised when the car turned into the car park of the Carlton Hotel on Park Lane. Caroline took them straight to reception and introduced them to the receptionist.

"This is Doctor Jose de Salvador, his wife Ellinor de Salvador and their daughter Emma Sinead. They will stay in Mr Andrusanke's suite for the next three days, can you please make sure they taken care of."

"Yes, of course," the receptionist replied.

Caroline turned to the family, "Have a great time in London and for you, Emma Sinead, here is your list and I expect you to visit every place written on the paper. I will see you back here in three days, but I will contact you before I leave Brighton." Emma Sinead was excited at spending three whole days in London! She never imagined this would ever happen to her. Her Dream nearly came true as she stood outside Buckingham Palace, watching the Royal family returning from the Trooping of the Colour. She held her mother's arm and joked, "Mama, maybe the Queen will see us and invite us to tea." Her mother laughed and thought, "If only she knew, her dream could very well come true!" The Salvador family visited all the places on the list that Caroline had given Emma Sinead.

The three days flew by quickly and all too soon, Caroline collected them as arranged.

Back at the Belmont Hotel next morning, Emma Sinead was first down to the reception and could not wait to tell everyone of her exciting three days.

As she was telling the receptionist about her holiday in London, she noticed a head appear from round the corner. "Isaac," she called out, "I have so much I have to tell you." She turned to the receptionist and asked, "May I take Isaac over to the lounge seats?"

The receptionist explained, "Mr Andrusanke left instructions that if Isaac was causing a problem he would have to go to the apartment."

"Please," Emma Sinead replied, "he just wants to know all about my adventure in London."

"Well," replied the receptionist, "In that case, I am sure it will be ok." Emma Sinead took hold of Issac's collar, "Come along, Isaac."

The receptionist watched as Emma Sinead walked across the lounge, Isaac walking beside her wagging his tail.

The guests leaving the hotel commented to the receptionist, about the pretty young girl in the corner talking to an Irish Red Setter in Spanish.

The receptionist just laughed, "I think the dog is having Spanish lessons." About 30 minutes later Jose and Ellinor appeared. He spoke to the receptionist.

"Excuse me have you seen our daughter?"

"Yes!" she replied, "she is over there," pointing over towards where Emma Sinead was sitting, "giving her new friend Isaac, Spanish lessons."

They both looked over, to see Isaac sitting bolt upright paying complete and rapt attention to what Emma Sinead was saying.

Ellinor de Salvador walked over and said, "Emma Sinead, I am not too sure if Isaac understands Spanish."

"Yes he does Mama," replied Emma Sinead, she then spoke in Spanish to Isaac, "*Acuestece senor Isaac*", and without hesitation, Isaac lay down.

"Very good," replied her mother.

Jose spoke, "Return Isaac to the reception area now Emma Sinead and we will go and have breakfast."

Emma Sinead looked at Isaac and in Spanish said, "*Sr. Isaac debe volver ahora a la zona de recepcion.*" Both Jose and Ellinor were lost for words as Isaac stood up and walked slowly over to reception, then stood peering out from behind the reception counter and as if nothing strange had happened. Emma Sinead looked at her mother and father and said, "Ok Papa, Mama let's go and eat."

As Jose passed the receptionist he commented, "I didn't know Isaac understood Spanish." The receptionist replied, "He's only had a thirty minute lesson from your daughter."

Over breakfast, Jose told his wife that he was going to London with an English surgeon he met at the conference, to spend some time in a children's hospital. "What will you and Emma Sinead do?" he asked.

"We will take a tour round the shops of Brighton and look for some little gifts for our friends," Ellinor answered.

"I think we will be going by train to Kings Cross station. I believe it's the centre of London." As Doctor Jose spoke, there was a tap on his shoulder. "Good morning, Dr. de Salvador," a voice said. Then Jose turned round, "Hello Dr Darren, are you ready to go now? Let me introduce you. This is my wife, Ellinor and my daughter Emma Sinead."

"I'm pleased to meet you both," Dr Darren said as he shook Ellinor's hand. Then looking at Emma Sinead he commented, "Your father told me you are a clever girl but he failed to mention that you were so pretty, in fact, he never stops talking about you." Emma Sinead blushed, then gave her father a big hug.

"Thank you, Papa" she said.

Giving his wife a kiss on the cheek and a big hug to Emma Sinead he said, "We must go now."

On their way to their room Emma Sinead poked her head round the reception desk and spoke in Spanish to Isaac. "*Sea usted un buen perro y voy a volver mas tarde.*"

The receptionist commented, "I am sure Isaac understands Spanish, since you came into this Hotel Emma Sinead, he is a different dog."

Chapter 13

Dr. de Salvador's visit to the children's hospital was enlightening, and left him with a good impression of the care the children received. After a quick lunch with some of the doctors in the hospital, he left and made his way towards the underground station. He looked up at the train map in the station and realised that he was close to Oxford Street and Bond Street. Deciding there was plenty of time, he could stroll round and see if he could buy a birthday present for Emma Sinead.

With her birthday in only two days, he had no idea what to get her. Wandering down Oxford Street, he could see nothing that inspired him. As he approached Oxford Circus underground station, he looked up, saw the name Baker Street, and immediately remembered his old books and the stories about Sherlock Holmes and doctor Watson. He even remembered the number 221B Baker Street. "I wonder if it's still there?" he thought.

He took the underground train to Baker Street and walked through the exit to the street above. As he strolled along towards 221B, he came to a large building which looked as if it had once been a church or a place of worship. It now housed two small shops, one of which was a jewellery shop. He stopped and looked in the window and decided on a whim, to go inside.

"Good afternoon sir, may I help you?" enquired the young man behind the counter.

"I am not sure," replied Jose, "I'm just walking around trying to find inspiration for a birthday present for my daughter."

"How old is your daughter sir?" asked the young man. "She will be thirteen years old in a few days," answered Jose. "Perhaps a little locket or a brooch?" the assistant replied, as he reached for some boxes under the counter. He took out some small pieces of jewellery and placed them on the glass counter. Jose looked, but did not seem too impressed. He pointed to a necklace with four different coloured stones in a circle and one large glass stone set in the middle. The young assistant removed the necklace and as he handed it to Jose he commented, "It's a beautiful piece sir, fit for a princess."

"What would the cost of this be?" he enquired.

"I am not sure," replied the assistant, "it's been here for a number of years, but has never excited any interest. If you could please wait a moment sir, I will go and fetch the owner." Placing the necklace back in its box, he left and walked through a little doorway at the back of the shop.

A few moments later he returned, followed by a tall grey-haired man. "You were asking about a gift for your daughter's birthday, may I know her name sir?" the grey-haired man asked.

"Her name is Emma Sinead de Salvador." Jose replied.

"What a lovely name. I am sure she is very special to you and your wife, oh' sorry, I presume you are married," the old man said.

"Yes, I am married sir, my wife's name is Ellinor."

The old man continued. "The name Emma Sinead, that would be an old Celtic Germanic name, but your surname is Spanish, are you from Spain sir?" he enquired, "No," replied Jose, "I am from Argentina."

"What a beautiful country," the old man said, as he opened the gold embossed jewelled box. "This piece of jewellery sir, is a necklace of birthstones: The centrepiece being a white diamond, which of course, is your daughter's birthstone." He handed the opened box to Jose. He looked carefully at the necklace. "It's beautiful," he remarked, "but I'm afraid it would be too costly for me." He handed the box and necklace back to the old man, who glanced over to his young assistant, smiled, and then turned towards Jose without hesitating and reached out with the box in his hand. "Doctor de Salvador, let this be a special gift to your daughter on her birthday, there is no charge."

"I am sorry," said Jose, not reaching for the box and shaking his head, "I cannot accept it as a gift."

The old man smiled. "If you insist," he said. He paused, looked at Jose and continued, "I will make a trade with you Doctor de Salvador: You keep the necklace and when you return to Buenos Aries, give a little donation to your special church."

Jose thought for a minute then said, "I would be willingly to do that."

The old man handed the box to his young assistant." Gift wrap this for the good doctor." As he walked towards the rear of the shop, in a low voice said, "I know she will like her present." The young assistant covered the box in special birthday wrapping paper, and handed it to Jose. They talked for a few more minutes and as he left the shop, he turned round. The old man bowed and gave a little smile. Jose stepped outside into the afternoon sunshine and was taken by surprise, to see a taxi waiting with its door opened. "Kings Cross Station sir?" the driver asked, "yes, of course," replied the surprised Dr Jose.

That evening in the Hotel Belmont, Emma Sinead decided to stay in her room and use the Internet while her father and mother went to the restaurant. During dinner, Jose told his wife that he had a gift for Emma Sinead's birthday and reached into the inside pocket of his jacket for the package. He very carefully removed the outer wrapping paper and handed the box to his wife. She opened the outer box "My God!" she said. "It's beautiful!" as she looked at the gold embossed case with strange writing across the front. "It's so lovely," she remarked. "What does the writing say?"

Jose took the case from her hand, "Sorry," he said, "I didn't notice any writing on it in the shop." Now a little confused, "I was sure there was nothing written on the case when I saw it in the shop." He looked carefully at the writing. "I do not understand this language some words are in Latin and some are something else." He then handed the case back to his wife, "Wait until you see what's inside!" he breathed.

She carefully opened the case. "Oh my God it is beautiful," she said. Touching the centre stone, she asked, "Is it a real diamond?"

Jose answered, "The old man told me it is a real diamond and it's her birthstone."

"This must have been very expensive," Ellinor said, in awe. Jose explained what the old man had said about a donation to his special church in Buenos Aries.

"I already know which church he is talking about," Ellinor replied.

Jose interrupted her, "Wait a minute, I never told him I was a doctor, or that we came from Buenos Aries! I just said Argentina, and he knew my name."

"You must have my dear," his wife answered, "you just forgot."

"No, I did not forget," Jose replied. He continued, "Remember on

53

Christmas Eve, I told Emma Sinead we were going to a very special church. This is strange. The old man in the shop said those same words: Our special church. And when I walked out of the shop, there was a taxi waiting to take me to Kings Cross station, but I never ordered one." Ellinor pondered for a moment, "I would like the opportunity to meet with this gentleman," she said. "Maybe we could return to London. It would be nice to take Emma Sinead to the shop wearing her necklace, and show the shop owner how much we appreciate the gift."

"That sounds like a good idea," replied Jose.

Just as they finished their meal, the hotel owner, Alex Andrusanke, greeted them. "Doctor and Mrs de Salvador, I do hope you are enjoying your stay with us. I must apologize for not greeting you before, I have been away and just returned today, and of course doctor, your conference now over, you can relax and enjoy our beautiful spring weather." They invited Alex to join them, he sat down and talked for hours as if they had known each other for years. Ellinor told Alex the history of her family and the dramatic events after the birth of Emma Sinead. Alex Andrusanke talked of his life in the Soviet Union and of his grandfather from Ireland, who fought in the Russian revolution and why his grandfather had changed his name to Andrusanke. He also talked about his marriage to Nadia and the birth of his daughter Nikita, also when and why they left the Ukraine.

Then Alex said, "You mentioned to me Ellinor, about your family ties in Ireland and your daughter's wish to go there."

"Yes," replied Ellinor, "It may sound silly to you. Emma Sinead would like to return a little lock of hair belonging to her late great-grandfather, to his birthplace in Ireland."

"Where in Ireland is his birthplace?" Asked Alex.

Ellinor reached into her bag, pulled out a piece of paper, handed it to Alex and commented, "I am not sure how to pronounce the name."

Alex looked at the paper, but not wanting to say too much replied, "What a coincidence. I have just recently bought a small hotel in that village. "Please leave this with me for a few days, maybe I can organise something."

Just then, Alex's daughter Nikita came over, and after apologising for interrupting their meal, she introduced herself to Doctor Jose and Ellinor.

She spoke to her father, "Father have you seen Isaac? He's vanished off

54

the planet. He's not in reception or the house."

"Have you looked in my apartment?" he asked. "Yes father, I looked, and he's not there."

"Ok, don't worry," he said, "I'll organise a search party. I'm sure he's around somewhere."

"Excuse me, doctor and Mrs de Salvador," Nikita said, "I have to go and look for an elusive Irish Red Setter."

"I do hope you find him," replied Ellinor, as Nikita walked back towards the lift.

Jose spoke, "Alex, you have to organise a search party for a Red Setter and I think we will retire for the night."

"Yes," replied Alex, "I had better go dog hunting!"

Jose and his wife walked towards the lift and headed for the penthouse. As they exited the lift and rounded the corridor leading to the penthouse, they were greeted by a vicious growl. Ellinor spoke, "Isaac! What are you doing here?" as they approached, he recognised them and started to wag his tail. Jose had to step over him to open the door. Isaac had no intention of moving, as the door opened Emma Sinead greeted them.

Ellinor asked, "Emma Sinead, did you know that Isaac was outside your door all the time?"

"No Mama, I never knew," she replied. While they were talking, Jose telephoned reception.

"Excuse me, could you tell Miss Nikita that Isaac is sitting outside the penthouse door?" A few moments later, Nikita and her father appeared. Nikita spoke, "Isaac what are you doing here? Are you on guard duty or just hiding?" Isaac just sat there wagging his tail. The night porter came along the corridor and spoke to Nikita, "Excuse me miss, I came up here earlier and Isaac wouldn't let me pass." Alex looked at Isaac, "What's wrong with you?" Then Emma Sinead reached down and gave Isaac a big hug, then spoke to him in Spanish, "*Isaac, le agradezco que custodiaban ahora puede volver a la zona recepcion,*" and to their amazement, Isaac just walked away wagging his tail and returned to the reception area.

"Emma Sinead, what did you say to him?" asked Alex.

She responded, "I thanked him for looking after me and told him he could now return to the reception."

"Ok," Alex laughed. "Now we know he has been on guard duty!"

Nikita thanked Emma Sinead and said, "I worry when he is not around, in case he goes out the main door."

"He would never do that," Emma Sinead said. "He does not like to be outside on his own."

"You formed a special friendship with Isaac," said Alex. "He will miss you when you go home."

"I will always be in his heart," she answered.

Alex laughed and said, "Case closed, let everyone now retire for the night."

As Nikita and her father reached the reception area, Nikita spoke, "Father, I would like to see if what Emma Sinead said about Isaac is true." She opened the front doors wide and called Isaac over towards the door. Isaac responded immediately, walking slowly to the open doors and sat down as if to say, "I'm not going out there." Then, looking all round, he sauntered back to reception.

Chapter 14

Nikita arose early and decided to enjoy the early morning sunshine and walk from her home to the Hotel Belmont. "Good morning Miss Nikita," the receptionist greeted her.

"Good morning," replied Nikita. "Can you tell me if my father is in the Hotel?"

"Yes, I believe he's in the breakfast room having breakfast," replied the receptionist. Nikita walked through the large double doors and made her way to the end of the breakfast room where her father was sitting." Good morning my dear," Alex said. "Have you come to join me for breakfast?"

"I'll just have a coffee please, father," replied Nikita. "I need to be in Heathrow by lunchtime."

"Sorry my dear, I forgot your friends are arriving today. I think it would be best to leave within the hour if you are to avoid the traffic on the M25. I can get Caroline to take you there as she is not busy today."

"That's alright, father," replied Nikita. "I'm not sure how long I will have to wait, and you know what these commercial flights can be like."

She drank her coffee quickly. "OK father, I must go."

"Drive carefully my dear, I'll prepare the Hotel for the turmoil when the girls arrive!" Nikita laughed as she went out the door.

On arrival at the airport, Nikita was happy to see Saya sitting in the waiting area, talking on her mobile phone. "Hi Saya, sorry I'm late."

"Nikita, it's so good to see you!" Saya stood up and gave Nikita the traditional Japanese bow and a hug. "Please wait a moment, let me tell my parents you have arrived." She spoke briefly in Japanese and turned off her phone. "Now they are happy that you have arrived," she said.

Nikita spoke, "Alessia and Andrea are arriving at terminal one, I think around quarter past one. Both are coming from Spain as Alessia has been staying with Andrea for the past week."

Holding Saya's hand Nikita asked, "How was your flight?"

"The flight was ok. I went first to the USA for a few days to visit my cousin, and then caught a flight from Washington yesterday evening. And using all my charm at imigration here, I got through quickly." Nikita laughed, "I'm sure all you needed was a smile and they would let you in."

"Almost right," Saya said. Nikita reached down and picked up one of Saya's suitcases. "As we have time, let's put your luggage in my car, then we can walk over to terminal one. We may even have time for a coffee before they arrive." They walked to terminal one, and with one hour to spare, went direct to the coffee shop. Sitting at a table in a quiet corner, but with full view of the arrivals exit, Saya spoke, "Tell me all about this young girl. You think she is the fifth Princess?" Nikita began to explain all the coincidences that had taken place and the dream she'd had. "Saya! when you arrive at the hotel, you will feel her presence. It's the same feeling I had when I first met Andrea."

"Her name is Emma Sinead de Salvador, from Buenos Aries. But for now, we must let the gods do the work, we will treat her as a normal girl who's here on holiday."

"I understand, Nikita," replied Saya, "what is she like? Is she tall? Skinny?"

"She is tall, just like all of us and from what I found out, she is very intelligent and charming. By the way, Mr Isaac has taken a shine to her! He follows her everywhere she goes."

"Well," replied Saya, "that's a good sign for a start. I am so looking forward to meeting her."

"We will know for sure tomorrow night, father has organised a special secret birthday party for her. I believe her father will also give her the jewelled necklace."

"Do her parents know about the necklace?" Saya asked.

"No," replied Nikita. "I believe Padre Alonso gave the necklace to her father two days ago, while he visited London."

As they talked, they were aware of a lot of laughter coming from the meeting area. Nikita spoke, "I think I know who that is! I would know that laugh anytime, it is Andrea!" They both looked towards the meeting area and sure enough, Alessia had overturned her suitcase, the contents strewn all over the floor. Andrea was in hysterics and could not stop laughing. Nikita and Saya walked over, "*Ciao, Hola.*" Andrea did not see or hear Nikita or Saya.

Suddenly she looked up. "Nikita! Saya!" she blurted out. Alessia's face was bright red and all her clothes were on the ground in full view of everyone. Nikita and Saya helped to get all her clothes back in the suitcase, attracting the attention of many people who could not help but notice four tall, beautiful girls, all on their hands and knees. The four girls walked to the car park at terminal three, Andrea still in a state of laughter.

As she drove to Brighton, Nikita explained everything that had happened, and to the best of her knowledge, what might happen over the next few days.

That evening, while the Salvador family were having dinner, they could see Nikita and her friends in the reception. Ellinor realised that one of the girls was speaking in Italian to Isaac, but before she could comment to her husband, Alex Andrusanke arrived. "I hope you are all enjoying yourselves," he said, "especially you, Emma Sinead, after all, this is your dream holiday."

"We are having a wonderful time," replied Jose.

"Well," answered Alex, "Nikita has just returned from Heathrow with her friends, and I am afraid the peace and quiet of the Belmont Hotel has now officially ended!"

"I look forward to meeting with them," replied Jose. Emma Sinead said nothing. Just smiled.

Chapter 15

April 2, Ellinor woke early. She opened the curtains on the lounge windows and gazed out at a deep blue sea and not a cloud in the sky. A good day for a birthday, she thought. Just then Emma Sinead appeared. Ellinor greeted her with a big hug. "Happy birthday, my dear."

"Thank you, Mama," Emma Sinead replied. "So much is happening, I forgot my birthday."

"*Hola mi princesa compleanos.*"

"Papa!" Emma Sinead exclaimed. "You are in England now and you must speak English."

Her mother spoke, "I remember every minute and every second when you were born, and look at you now, thirteen years old! It's difficult to imagine how time has flown by." The telephone rang, Jose picked it up. After a moment he said, "Thank you very much, I will pass the phone to her right now."

"It's a call for you Emma Sinead." He handed the telephone to her. As she took the phone from her father's hand, she had a surprised look on her face. She spoke in a soft voice, "Hello?"

"Emma Sinead." Her grandmother said. "*La Abuela que eres tu. Abuela tengo tantas cosas que decirte que es tan emocionante.*"

"Grandmama! I am so happy to hear from you. I have lots to tell you." Emma Sinead told her Grandmama all about the possible trip to Ireland. Her grandmother, who was now very emotional, said, "I just knew it would happen. I know now, your great grandpa will be smiling. Emma Sinead, have a wonderful day! It is hard to imagine you are thirteen years old to the day."

"Thank you, Grandmama," Emma Sinead replied, "would you like to speak to Mama?"

"Yes please," her grandmother answered.

Ellinor greeted her mother in Spanish and spoke for some time, but was careful not to talk about the gift they had got for of Emma Sinead.

At that moment, Emma Sinead looked out of the large window towards the promenade. "Mama, Papa, look!"

"What's happening?" her mother asked. "Look, it's Isaac! He's running with the four girls."

"Are you sure that's Isaac?" her father asked as he looked out the window.

"Yes, I'm sure," said Emma Sinead. "That's Nikita in front with Isaac, and the other girls are her friends." Her mother looked out the window and commented, "Look how tall they all are, just like you Emma Sinead."

"I'm not that tall, Mama."

"You will be, you are still growing," her mother replied.

Jose came over to the window. "I like to see people jogging and keeping fit," he remarked.

Emma Sinead spoke, "Papa, is Grandmama still on the phone?"

"Oh yes," he replied, "I nearly forgot! Anabella, are you still there?"

"Yes, I am still here Jose. What's happening?"

He replied, "It was Emma Sinead calling us to the window. I'll pass the phone to her, and she can explain." As he handed the phone to Emma Sinead, his wife called from the kitchen. "Would you like coffee, Jose?"

"Yes please," he answered as he walked into the kitchen.

"Grandmama, I have something to tell you," Emma Sinead said speaking very quietly, "remember the dream I told you about."

"Yes, I remember, I still have your sketch," replied her grandmother. "Grandmama," she said in a low voice, "they're here!"

"What do you mean? Who is there?" her grandmother asked. "My four friends. The girls I saw in my dream. Remember, I told you about them."

"Are you sure they are the same girls?" her grandmother asked. "Yes Grandmama, they are the same girls, and they all speak different languages. I will send you a photograph of the girls from my Ipad."

"Please do, I am so happy for you my dear," said her grandmother. "I will talk to you later, go now and enjoy your birthday, bye bye."

Meanwhile, in the kitchen, Ellinor mentioned to her husband, "Do you remember when Nikita came into the dining room, yesterday evening?"

"Was that when she arrived with her friends?" asked Jose.

"Yes! And did you notice, when one of the girls was making a fuss of Isaac, she was speaking in Italian."

"No, I didn't notice," replied Jose.

Ellinor spoke, "I am reminded of the letter from Padre Matthew. Remember what it said, one Russian, one Italian."

Jose laughed. "Let's see if the other two are Spanish and Japanese. Then we will have a mystery!"

Ellinor called out, "Emma Sinead! It's time to get breakfast, come along."

"Coming Mama!" she called out from the bedroom. They made their way down to the dining room. When they reached the reception desk, there was Isaac, looking like a happy red setter, wagging his tail like a propeller and panting like a steam engine. Emma Sinead looked at Isaac. "Poor Isaac," she said as she stroked him, "you look so tired." The receptionist spoke, "Emma Sinead, he is just happy to see you and of course, he has been running on the promenade with Miss Nikita." Then hugging Isaac, Emma Sinead said, "I will see you later Isaac, after you have had a rest."

Alex Andrusanke walked in. "Good morning, *Buon compleanno di Emma Sinead*." Taken by surprise, Emma Sinead answered in Spanish, "*Si parla spagnolo Mr Andrusanke*."

"No No," he replied. "My daughter's friend Andrea is from Spain, and she has been teaching me." On hearing 'Spain', Jose looked at his wife. There was a smile on her face.

"I say it better in Russian." "*С Днем Рождения Мисс Эмма Шинед*. And as it is a very special day for you, Emma Sinead, we are going to allow you to take Isaac for his afternoon walk along the promenade."

"Wow!" she looked to her mother, "Mama, this is great! Can we walk with Isaac? This is going to be the best birthday ever!"

"It's a lovely day, we can take him after lunch," Ellinor answered.

They finished breakfast and returned to the penthouse, where they spent the rest of the morning. Emma Sinead had connected her Ipad to the internet and was talking to her friends from her school. Ellinor spoke quietly to her husband, "I think we have a mystery, my dear."

"I think you are right!" he answered in a soft voice. "Let's wait and see if the last girl is Japanese."

A voice from the bedroom called out, "She is from Tokyo, and her name is Saya." Jose had just picked up the phone to call his colleague in Buenos Aries. He replaced the phone when he heard his daughter's remark.

"How do you know that?" her mother asked, "I just know," was Emma Sinead's candid reply.

Ellinor looked at her husband and whispered, "We need to talk!"

"Right," said Jose, "let's go to the lounge." He called to Emma Sinead, "Your mother and I are going down to the lounge for a moment."

"Ok Papa, I will remain here." Jose and Ellinor entered the lounge through the large double doors and walked to the far end, well away from other people.

Ellinor spoke first, "Jose, I am worried for Emma Sinead. Remember we laughed, when she talked about her four imaginary friends, now I think they are real and here in the hotel."

"You mean the four girls?"

"Yes," she replied.

"Ellinor, I know some odd things have happened, are they nothing more than coincidences? Why not talk with your mother and tell her your concerns? I am sure Anabella knows more than she is telling us."

"Ok, I will do that later," Ellinor replied. They made their way back to the penthouse. As they entered, Ellinor spoke, "Emma Sinead, it is time to take Isaac for his walk."

They went down to reception and as usual, Isaac was there to greet Emma Sinead, tail wagging at full speed. The receptionist had his lead ready and instructed Emma Sinead, "On no account let him off the lead as he likes to chase seagulls!"

"I promise," replied Emma Sinead. She held the lead tightly as they walked out of the hotel. Her mother, father and Isaac, with his head high trotting alongside her.

The receptionist commented to Mr Andrusanke, "I am amazed to see Isaac behave so well with a complete stranger." Alex replied as he walked away, "Isaac knows who she is."

The Salvador family spent two hours walking Isaac along the seafront before returning to the hotel.

"I got lots of photographs," Emma Sinead said to the receptionist, "and Mama took some shots of me with Isaac. I can now send them to my friends in school."

"I think Isaac will miss you when you go home," said the receptionist.

"They will miss each other," answered Ellinor.

Emma Sinead handed the lead to the receptionist and said, "I think he needs a drink of water now, he seems very thirsty." The receptionist took Isaac through the hallway and handed him over to the day porter. "Can you make sure he has some water to drink, and then bring him back to the reception area."

"Yes ma'm," he replied.

That evening, they dressed especially nicely for dinner. The doctor had booked their table for 9pm, unaware that his plans had been changed by Alex. Both just sat relaxing, as usual, Emma Sinead was on her Ipad talking to some of her school friends in Buenos Aires. Jose heard a noise outside their door.

"Did you hear that?" he asked.

"No, I heard nothing," replied Ellinor. "Listen, there it is again! Sounds like a dog," he said.

Emma Sinead jumped up from her chair and ran to the door. Before she even opened it, she shouted, "It's Isaac!" As she stepped out into the hallway, Isaac ran a little way down the hall, barked and stopped.

"What's the matter Isaac?" she said. He ran a little more, and again stopped.

"Mama, I think Isaac wants us to follow him!" said Emma Sinead. Her mother looked at her husband. "Maybe there's a fire?"

"Of course not, we would have heard the alarms," he remarked. He continued, "Isaac has just come to see Emma Sinead."

"No, Papa," Emma Sinead replied. "When I walk towards him, he runs ahead, he is expecting us to follow him."

"Ok," Jose said, "maybe my watch is wrong and Isaac is right. Let's all follow the leader, it's nearly 9pm now." As they walked out of the penthouse door, Isaac stood up and started to walk ahead, stopping and looking back just to make sure they were following. Isaac knew he could not go in the lift, he ran down the stairs ahead of them as fast as he could, all three followed. When they got to reception, it was eerily quiet, not a soul in sight. Jose pointed to the big sign, written in Spanish, on the dining room door it read, '*Habitacion Senorita Sineads Cumpleanos.*'

"It's your birthday room, Emma Sinead," said her father. She opened the door slowly and peeked inside. The room was dark but she could see the outline of people sitting at tables. Suddenly, all the lights came on, there was a big applause and everyone started to sing, 'Happy Birthday'. Jose and Ellinor were completely surprised and slowly entered the room. Alex approached, took Emma Sinead by the hand and spoke, "Ladies and Gentlemen tonight we celebrate the 13th birthday of this beautiful lady from Buenos Aries in Argentina." Everyone applauded as Alex guided her to a table in the centre of the dining hall and then beckoned her parents to join her. Just as they sat at the table, Nikita came to their table and wished Emma Sinead a happy birthday. She then introduced her three friends one by one.

"This is Alessia from Sorrento in Italy, Andrea from Santiago de Compostela in Spain and Saya from Tokyo Japan." Ellinor suddenly remembered a programme on television about a young Japanese mountain climber.

"Excuse me, Saya," she asked, are you the girl that climbs mountains without ropes? I have seen a programme on television recently."

"Yes," replied Saya. "It's one of my hobbies and last year the television company wanted to make a film of me climbing."

"Is it not dangerous?" Ellinor asked.

"I suppose it is," replied Saya, "but when I am climbing I don't think of that, my only thoughts are the top of the mountain."

During the meal, Emma Sinead said to her mother, "Mama do you like Miss Nikita's friends?"

"They are so beautiful and behave like sisters," her mother replied.

"Yes, they are Mama," Emma Sinead answered.

After dinner, Jose handed Emma Sinead a package. He spoke softly, "This is our gift to you, on your 13th birthday." Ellinor looked on, with a big smile on her face, there was silence in the room as she opened the package.

"Oh Mama! Papa! It is beautiful! It's just like the necklace in my dream!

Wait until I tell Grandmama." Ellinor reached over, "Here, let me help you put it on." As she placed the necklace around her neck, she was sure the stones gave a little flash of green light.

Her father explained to her, "The stone in the middle is your birth stone, and we think the other four are also birth stones, but we are not sure."

"They are Papa," Emma Sinead answered.

Saya, sitting with her three friends, spoke in a soft whisper, "She is the one."

Alessia nodded, "I know, she is the Fifth princess."

"Yes, she is," answered Nikita.

Andrea laughed and remarked, "Soon, no more airline tickets."

Nikita answered Andrea's remark, "Andrea, we must be careful what we say when we meet this girl."

Alex stood up. "It's a custom in the Ukraine, for the birthday girl to walk round the tables to receive her birthday greeting from all the guests." He invited Jose and Ellinor to walk their daughter round to each table. As they reached the end table, where Nikita and her friends were sitting, each of the girls, in turn, gave Emma Sinead a kiss on the cheek and wished her a happy birthday. Andrea spoke to Emma Sinead in Spanish, "*Your father and mother's gift is very beautiful.*"

"Thank you," replied Emma Sinead, "I think today, my whole life has changed."

Ellinor could not understand why she suddenly felt a great wave of emotion. Before they walked back to their table, Ellinor took a photograph with Emma Sinead's Ipad, of the girls and Emma Sinead. As they walked back to their table and sat down, Alex and his wife came over, and Alex introduced his wife to the Salvador family. "This is my wife Nadia, she has been to see her friends in the Ukraine and just arrived back today."

"Please sit here with us," Ellinor said, as she beckoned her to sit down. As she sat down, she commented on how tall Emma Sinead was.

"The height always seems to come from the mother," answered Alex, "but the looks always come from the man!" he laughed.

"Thank God you are only telling one lie," replied Nadia. She then followed with, "It's the second one," she said smiling.

"Ladies and gentleman!" Alex said, in a loud booming voice, two of my daughter's friends, Alessia and Andrea are not only beautiful, but are also talented musicians. They are going to entertain us for the next hour. So, let me introduce you all, to Alessia del Amato from Sorrento in Italy, and Andrea De Silva from Santiago de Compostela in Spain." Both girls stood up, Andrea walked to the piano and Alessia picked up the guitar. It was when they stood side by side that Jose and Ellinor realised how tall they were. She held her husband's arm tightly. He looked at her, "You have a tear in your eye," he said tenderly, "are you sad?"

"No," she replied, "I am happy. Emma Sinead could not have had a better birthday." Ellinor decided to ring her mother and Padre Matthew next day.

"This cannot be just a coincidence," she thought.

Just then, Andrea spoke in English with a soft Spanish accent, "I love music, and I usually like to sing songs that I have written. But tonight the song will be, Bridge over Troubled Water. This is specially for Emma Sinead. Because we live in a world of turmoil and conflicts, it is up to all of us not only to build bridges, but we must make the effort to walk across them."

The two girls began the music and their singing resonated throughout the room. As they finished, there was a moment of silence before everyone stood up and applauded. "Mama," Emma Sinead said, "are you sad?"

"No, I am not sad my dear. The song was so emotional and beautiful."

Alex stood up. "Ladies and gentlemen, we have not finished yet!" He took Emma Sinead by the hand, and walked with her to the centre of the dining hall. The door to the kitchen opened and the chef walked out, followed by all the kitchen staff carrying a large cake, with thirteen lighted candles. They placed it on the table in the middle of the dining hall.

"Emma Sinead de Salvador the honour is yours," he called out. "Jose and Ellinor, please come to the table and help your daughter to honour us, by blowing out the candles." After she had blown out the candles and cut the first slice, Andrea, speaking in Spanish was the first to wish her a happy birthday. Next was Alessia, who spoke Italian, then Saya who spoke Japanese, and finally Nikita, who spoke in Russian.

Alex stood up and tapped the table, and when he knew he had everyone's attention he spoke. "Tonight, we celebrate the 13th birthday of a young lady from Buenos Aries in Argentina. The Salvador family have been guests of this hotel for the past two weeks, and I believe on their return to Argentina, they will take back many fond memories of their time with us, in the United Kingdom." When Alex had finished, Jose stood up to speak, tapping the table with a spoon. "May I have your attention please, when we came here to the United Kingdom, it was for a medical conference. My family and I never expected to be treated as part of a large family. We find it difficult to comprehend everything that has taken place. I know Emma Sinead will never forget this moment for the rest of her life. I say thank you! To all the Hotel staff, to the four beautiful ladies, for the welcome that you have all afforded to my daughter. Very special thanks to Alex Andrusanke and his lovely wife Nadia, and of course, we cannot forget one member of staff, Isaac, for being a very special friend to my daughter." He continued, "Almost thirteen years ago, to this day, in the University Hospital in Buenos Aries, a complete stranger said to my wife, your daughter is very special! Well! If I met that person right now, I would say to him, you were so right all those years ago!"

Then Jose raised his glass, "To you, Alex Andrusanke, your wife Nadia, Nikita and her three friends, all the hotel staff and to my lovely wife and daughter."

Nikita looked at the three girls and in a low voice said, "The Fifth princess has arrived."

Chapter 16

The following day Jose, Ellinor and Emma Sinead got the early train to London, to visit the shop where Jose obtained Emma Sinead's necklace.

Arriving at Kings Cross station, he walked with his family down the escalator to the Underground station, and after studying the map, got on the circle line direct to Baker Street. They strolled slowly along the street, Jose pointed to the house 221B Baker Street where the famous Sherlock Holmes and Dr Watson had lived. Emma Sinead had to have her photograph taken, standing with her mother outside the house with the plaque clearly visible on the first floor.

"Papa," Emma Sinead said, "you stand here with Mama, and I will take the picture." After taking lots of photographs, they strolled down the street slowly. Jose had difficulties in finding the jewellery shop.

"Maybe it was in one of the side streets?" offered Ellinor.

"No, this is the correct street," he replied, "I am sure."

"Papa," Emma Sinead said, "you said it looked like an old church. Look over there!" as she pointed to two buildings. "It looks like the building," he said, but it's a clothing shop."

"Well, I think we should ask someone," Ellinor suggested. "Let's go and ask in that shop. It's part of the same building."

All three entered the shop and seeing a woman standing at the far end, the family approached her. "Excuse me," Jose said, "do you know where the jewellery shop is?"

"Wait a moment," the woman answered. "I'll ask my husband if he knows." Her husband came out from a side room, and shaking Jose's hand, spoke, "I recall someone telling me, there used to be a jewellery next door many years ago." He continued, "The builders divided the old church in two. The monks used to live in this part, and I believe the other half was the chapel."

The women reappeared carrying a photo frame. "I have no idea how old the picture is. It was on the wall when we came here," she said as she handed it to Jose. He and Ellinor looked at the photo. It showed four people standing outside the building, Ellinor looked shocked. "That's Padre Alonso," she said pointing to one of the figures in the photograph.

"He also looks like the old gentleman in the jewellery shop!" Jose exclaimed. "But how can that be?"

The woman's husband spoke, "I'm sorry that's all we know. I can give you a copy of the photograph." He walked into the back of the shop and returned a few moments later and handed Jose the photocopy.

The Salvador family left the shop, both Jose and Ellinor in a state of shock. They made their way to Kings Cross Station arriving back at the Belmont hotel late evening and went straight to the dining room.

After lunch, Jose and Ellinor walked out of the dining room, leaving Emma Sinead in the lounge talking to Isaac. When they approached reception they could see Alex and Nadia there talking with Caroline. "Excuse me, Doctor Jose," Alex called out and beckoned for the doctor and his wife to come and join them.

Nadia spoke, "Ellinor, The Argentine Ambassador and a Mrs Cather-Jones from Buckingham Palace are coming here tomorrow to talk with you and Emma Sinead. Have you spoken to Emma Sinead yet about her meeting with the Queen?"

"You knew about this?" enquired the surprised doctor.

"Yes, we do know, and I can confirm now that Emma Sinead will meet with the Queen and Prince Phillip."

Jose replied, "We have not yet mentioned anything to our daughter."

"Well," said Nadia, "I would suggest you tell her before this meeting tomorrow, it will prepare her mentally."

Holding her husband's hand, Ellinor spoke softly, "I cannot believe this is happening!"

Nadia was quick to respond, "Ellinor, the selection of Emma Sinead for this task was because she is special." Ellinor was surprised by those words. She had heard those same words repeated to her many times since Emma Sinead was born. "I would suggest that you tell Emma Sinead this evening and tomorrow you and I will have a long talk."

Ellinor called to Emma Sinead, "It's time to say good night to Isaac." Emma Sinead gave Isaac a hug and said in Spanish, "*Isaac! lo siento pero tengo que ir ahora.*"

Isaac looked at her and sauntered back to the reception area.

Nikita came over with her friends and immediately Andrea and Emma Sinead were laughing and chattering away in Spanish.

"You see," commented Nikita, "Andrea never stops joking." She then called to Isaac, "Come along Isaac, time to go home." Jose and Ellinor made their way to the lift. "Emma Sinead, time to go!" her mother called out again.

When they reached the penthouse, Emma Sinead asked if she could use her Ipad. "Not at the moment," her mother said, "your father and I have something important to discuss with you."

"Am I in trouble, Mama?" asked Emma Sinead.

"Good heavens no," replied Ellinor. All three sat round the kitchen table. Emma Sinead had a look of apprehension on her face.

Her mother spoke, "Do you remember, a long time ago, when you were talking to me about having tea with the Queen?"

"Yes Mama, I was only joking!"

Her father looked at her, "Emma Sinead, it's no longer a joke."

"Papa, I only said that to make Mama laugh."

"Emma Sinead," her mother said, as she held the girl's hand, "It's true, you are going to meet with the Queen of England."

"Mama!" Emma Sinead said, "Now, you are joking."

Her father looked at her and smiled. "Emma Sinead, we are not joking. Your wish is going to come true." He went on to explain everything, and told her about the people arriving at the Hotel tomorrow.

"I do not want you to worry and be nervous, we could not tell you sooner," her mother said as she hugged her.

"Mama, I won't be nervous," Emma Sinead replied, "I will just be Emma Sinead de Salvador." Her mother reached over and put her arm round her daughter. "My God!" she said, "You are indeed special!" As she put her arm round her she noticed that the five stones on the necklace round Emma Sinead's neck seemed to be a pale bright green. Ellinor spoke to her husband, "Look at Emma Sinead's necklace! It is shining." Jose looked.

"Yes, it looks a little brighter, perhaps the lights in here are affecting the stones."

"Papa, Mama," Emma Sinead responded, "they become brighter when I am near the four girls, and Mama, they all have necklaces like mine."

"Time for bed now my dear, it's late, and please, Emma Sinead, you must not mention what we have talked about to anyone! Especially on your Ipad."

"Can I tell Grandmama?" she asked.

Her father interrupted her, "Emma Sinead, you must not tell anyone until you have permission to do so. It's because of security."

"Mama, I will not talk about it to anyone! I promise. Good night mama, good night papa," said Emma Sinead, as Ellinor and Jose walked out of her bedroom.

"Well!" said Ellinor, "I hope she will not worry about the meeting with the Queen."

Jose replied, "Her grandmother always said that she is just like her great grandmother, Isabel! No panic, she just takes everything in her stride."

Ellinor asked, "Why do the girls have similar necklaces? What does it mean?"

"I think your mother can answer that question," replied Jose.

Chapter 17

The next morning, Nadia telephoned Ellinor and suggested they meet in the Hotel lounge after breakfast.

All three were sitting in the lounge when Nadia appeared. She sat down beside Emma Sinead, put her arm round her shoulder and said, "Well, Miss Emma Sinead, your big day is fast approaching. Are you looking forward to meeting the Queen?"

"Yes, I am, it will be a great experience," she answered. "But I do not understand. Why me?" she asked.

"Your father and mother will be the best people to explain everything to you later. Please remember that some people are coming here to meet with you today. One will be the Argentinean Ambassador, a man from the British Foreign Office, and a very nice lady from the Queens Household." She continued, "But now, I am going to take your mother away for a short while, to talk with her." "Nikita and her friends will keep you and your father company." Just as Nadia spoke, they could hear laughter coming from reception. "It sounds like the girls have arrived!" Nadia said.

Suddenly, Isaac came bounding in followed by the four girls. Wagging his tail like an airplane propeller, he made straight for Emma Sinead and calmly sat down beside her.

"I am so sorry mother, I know he's not allowed in the dining hall," apologised Nikita.

"Well, now that he is here he may as well stay," Nadia replied. "I would like you four girls to stay here and keep Emma Sinead and her father company, while I go and talk with Ellinor."

They both walked to Nadia's apartment. "Please," Nadia said, as she called to Ellinor, "sit by the large panoramic window, it's a beautiful view. I love to sit here and look out over the sea and just ponder on our lives."

Ellinor replied, "I am afraid with my job, looking after Jose and Emma Sinead, there is not much time for pondering." She continued, "Nadia, I worry, what if something was to happen to Jose or me? What would become of Emma Sinead?"

"Ellinor," answered Nadia, "we always worry about their future. Nothing will happen to you or your husband and please, do not worry about Emma Sinead, she will be fine." Nadia then said, "I know Ellinor when she was born, there were complications, but look at her now, tall, beautiful and very clever." Nadia paused for a moment, before she spoke again, "When I gave birth to Nikita, there were complications, just like Emma Sinead. I met someone who told me that Nikita was special. You know who I am talking about?"

"Was it Padre Alonso?" Ellinor asked incredulously.

"Yes, it was," replied Nadia.

"I don't understand," said Ellinor. "We were led to believe he had passed away many years ago."

"Ellinor, what I am about to tell you, is something your mother has known for a long time. God chose Padre Alonso to lead a mission to save humanity from its own destruction. That day by the lake, he sent two angels and they asked Padre Alonso to go with them." She continued, "Ellinor! Padre Alonso did not die, he became the servant of God destined to work with the angels. But even angels need a little help. God chose four girls, and gave them special powers, and sent Padre Alonso to search for the fifth and final one. You know who that is."

Nadia explained the history of the four girls and their connection to the ancient Celtic race and to Emma Sinead. She told Ellinor, when each of the girls reached the age of thirteen years, they received a gift of a special necklace, each having four stones in a circle and one in the middle. "We knew there would be five girls because there were five stones on each necklace. We also knew the Angels would give us a sign and they did. It was when Nikita saw your names on the hotel registry and then she had the dream just like your Emma Sinead. We believed then the fifth and future Princess would arrive on her thirteenth birthday." Nadia continued, "One year ago, when Emma Sinead would have been celebrating her twelfth birthday, Nikita came to me. She told me there was a fifth girl, but that was all she knew. Just after Christmas, when we first had the booking list for the conference, Nikita saw your husband's name on the list and further down the list, she saw both your name and that of Emma Sinead. She knew immediately! She told me she had a dream of a young girl holding her hand out and calling her. I asked her how could she be certain? She told me when she saw your family names on the list, she just knew Emma Sinead was the Fifth Princess."

Ellinor listened intently to every word and asked, "Why Emma Sinead? And why a Princess?" Nadia explained the five girls contribution to World Peace. The first step for Emma Sinead, will be the meeting with the Queen on behalf of her country. "Ellinor, we do not have much time today, and we should continue this conversation another day."

Jose was happy to remain in the lounge in the company of all the girls, and was content just to sit and listen to them talking. He was surprised how quickly Emma Sinead settled in. In fact, he thought, a complete stranger would think they were five sisters. At around 11:30, the receptionist walked over to Jose.

"Dr. de Salvador, there are four people at the reception desk wishing to speak with you and your wife."

Immediately, Nikita took charge. "I will go and fetch mother and Mrs de Salvador." Just as she was about to walk out of the lounge, her mother and Ellinor walked through the door followed by two men and two women. As they approached the group in the lounge, Nadia spoke, "Doctor de Salvador and Emma Sinead, let me introduce you to our guests. The Argentinean Ambassador to the United Kingdom, Ignacio de Castro and his secretary Maria Sanchez." Jose was by now standing beside Ellinor and Emma Sinead. The Ambassador shook their hands and commented, "I have seen your photograph Emma Sinead, but in real life, you look more stunning and beautiful and it is a great pleasure to meet with you."

"Thank you," replied Emma Sinead.

Nadia, stepping slightly to one side, then interrupted. "This is Mr Michael Hagen from the British Foreign Office, and this young lady is Michelle Carter-Jones from her Majesty the Queen's Secretarial Office." Nadia introduced her daughter Nikita and her friends, not forgetting Isaac, and then suggested to her guests that her office would be a more appropriate place to have their meeting. She asked her guests if they would like to have lunch at the Hotel. The offer was accepted and they walked towards the lift.

During the meeting, Michelle Carter-Jones suggested that Emma Sinead and her parents should travel to Windsor. This would enable Emma Sinead to have some tuition in Court etiquette and be more comfortable within the castle area. The Ambassador explained the reasons for the meeting, and told Ellinor that he would be collecting them on Friday morning at exactly ten fifteen and accompanying them to Windsor Castle. They needed to be there by twelve twenty at the latest.

The meeting lasted just over one hour. While walking to the dining hall, the Argentinean Ambassador spoke to Jose and Ellinor. "I am very impressed with your daughter's ability to communicate; sadly, it's lacking in many children of her age. She has impressed everyone in the room and I am quite satisfied that she is the correct choice."

Just as Nadia sat down, Alex arrived. Nadia introduced him to the Argentinean Ambassador, his secretary Maria Sanchez and Miss Michelle Carter-Jones. Alex had already met Michael Hagen from the British foreign office. "The meeting went well, I presume?" asked Alex. "Yes," the Ambassador answered, "I have great confidence in Emma Sinead and have no doubts about her ability to fulfil this mission." Alex turned to Emma Sinead, "You, young lady, will be frontpage news on every newspaper in the world in a few days, and your country will be so proud of you." Ellinor put her arm round her daughter, "I am so proud of her right now, I could not have wished for a better daughter."

"Oh dear, I forgot, there is someone important I want you to meet," Alex said to Emma Sinead, as he walked out of the dining hall towards reception. Emma Sinead, her mother and Jose sat there, wondering what or who was going to walk through the door with Alex. The door at the end of the dining hall opened slowly.

"Grandmama," shouted Emma Sinead, as she ran to greet her grandmother. Ellinor and Doctor Jose were more than surprised. As Anabella hugged Emma Sinead, she said, "I had to come, I missed you so much and I could not miss your big day." Jose looked at Alex. "How did you manage to arrange that?" he asked. "You have to thank the Ambassador and Mr Michael Hagen. They made all the arrangements," Alex replied, "I just collected Anabella at Gatwick Airport."

Chapter 18

Just before the Ambassador, his secretary and Mr Michael Hagen left the Belmont Hotel to return to London, Michael spoke with Alex in his office.

"Alex, you were right about the young Argentine girl, absolutely the correct choice, in fact I will organise that all five girls come to the palace."

"That is a very good decision," remarked Alex. "Lots of things are happening Michael regarding the five girls and you can expect an invitation one of these days to join us and see the magic of the Celts."

"Thank you, Alex, for all the work you have done for our country and I await that invitation. Now! I must not keep the ambassador waiting."

As Michael walked out of the office he turned to Alex, smiled and said, "They are just like five sisters."

The Salvador family travelled with Miss Michelle Carter Jones to Windsor, while Anabella rested in the Hotel after her long flight from Buenos Aries. Not expecting her family to return from Windsor until late in the evening, she wandered down to the Hotel lounge. As she sat there, watching the people walking around. She observed four girls entering the lounge from the dining hall. She immediately recognised the girls from the drawing and the photograph Emma Sinead had sent her through the internet. She stood up and walked towards the four girls, "You must be Nikita," she said.

"Yes, I am Nikita," was the reply. Anabella handed Nikita the drawing. "This is how I know you and your friends," she said. Nikita looked at the drawing, the three other girls peering over her shoulder.

"Look, that's me!" exclaimed Andrea, pointing to one of the figures, "and that looks like Saya!"

"Are you Emma Sinead's grandmother?" enquired Nikita. "The drawing is so life like, when did you do this?" Anabella explained how she got the drawing. "It's amazing!" said Saya, "and just from her Dream!"

"May we sit and talk with you?" asked Alessia.

"It would be an honour," replied Anabella, "I have waited a long time for this moment." The four girls sat down, Nikita was the first to speak. "How did you know about us, Mrs Fernandez?"

Anabella replied, "Please call me Anabella. In the beginning, I did not know how many children there were, and I had no idea whether they were boys or girls. I only knew there were some special people. It was after my daughter Ellinor, (Emma Sinead's mother) was born, I first met Padre Alonso. When he told me a fifth princess would be born, that is when I knew there were four girls. My father gave me the most compelling information, but at the time I had no reference to check from." Anabella looked at the four girls. "When I was a young girl living on our farm in Patagonia I used to think they were only stories when my father told me about five beautiful princesses. And now it is all happening."

The four girls all reached out and held Anabella's hand. Alessia spoke in her Italian accent, "Anabella, you are a wonderful lady and we are very fortunate to have met you." She continued, "All those years, you kept your belief and guided your grandaughter. She will very soon become the fifth princess, and fulfil your father's wish." Just at that moment, Alex came in. "I see you ladies have become acquainted!" Then he noticed a tear in Anabella's eye. "Are you all right, Anabella?" he asked. Anabella looked at him, "I have never been as happy in my whole life," she answered. "You, Alex, have a wonderful daughter, and she has wonderful friends. We are going to get along just fine."

The four girls left Anabella with Alex and returned to Nikita's house. Anabella and Alex sat in the lounge talking. Nadia entered the lounge, "I have ordered a light tea for everyone, and of course, coffee for you Anabella."

"Thank you, Nadia," said Anabella. "You have no idea how excited I am to be here, and to have met Nikita and her friends."

"It's a great pleasure to have you here," replied Nadia, "and of course, meeting with Emma Sinead and her parents is wonderful."

Alex and Anabella talked for hours and at round 21:30, Emma Sinead peered in the lounge door. "Grandmama!" she shouted, "you will never guess where we have been!" As she ran to the end of the lounge and hugged her grandmother.

"Are you not going to greet Mr and Mrs Andrusanke?" her grandmother asked.

"I am so sorry," she said, as she gave both a kiss on the cheek. Jose and Ellinor entered the lounge, followed by Isaac, who bounded straight to Emma Sinead.

"So, this is the famous Isaac!" Anabella remarked.

"Isn't he beautiful Grandmama?" said Emma Sinead.

Nadia spoke, "Since your grandaughter arrived at the Hotel, poor Isaac is not sure whether to follow Nikita or Emma Sinead."

Jose and Ellinor sat down, then Ellinor spoke. "Now, Emma Sinead, you may tell everyone about your adventure."

Emma Sinead went into detail about her experience. "First, we went to the offices and were introduced to everyone, then Miss Michelle Carter-Jones took us to the big room where we will meet the Queen. Grandmama, are you coming with us to meet the Queen?"

"I will be right behind you, child," replied her grandmother. "I would not miss this for the world."

"The Queen will think it is an Argentinean invasion," Jose laughed. He continued, "You realise, Emma Sinead, when you enter that room on Friday, not only will we be there, but so also will the Argentinean Ambassador and some Embassy staff, including members of the United Kingdom Foreign Office, and television cameras from around the world. Your photograph will be on every newspaper and TV channel in Argentina."

Anabella put her arm round the shoulder of her granddaughter, "I am so proud of you," she said, "your great-grandfather Thomas, and Isabel, your great-grandmother, will be with you every step of the way."

"My school friends will be surprised to see me on TV!" Emma Sinead said.

"I do believe your school will watching it live on TV," said her grandmother. "But Emma Sinead, you must not tell them. It will be a big surprise for them!"

"Grandmama, I am so excited to be meeting the Queen of England."

"Now, Emma Sinead, it is time for bed," said her mother. "A busy day tomorrow, and then the big day will be Friday." Alex turned to Jose, "As you will not be travelling to Windsor, you, I and the four girls would take a little trip."

As they walked from the lounge towards the lift, Anabella said to Emma Sinead, "I have a special surprise for you in my suitcase."

"Please tell me Grandmama, what's the surprise?"

Anabella answered, "It's something special, you will see in a moment."

When they entered the penthouse suite, Emma Sinead spoke in an excited voice,

"Can I see the surprise now Grandmama?"

Anabella took a large package from her suitcase and presented it to Emma Sinead. "This was made especially for you, by my tailor in Buenos Aries." As she handed the package to Emma Sinead, she said "Take this to your room and come out wearing it. I want to see a real princess."

While Emma Sinead was in her room, Anabella sat down with Jose and Ellinor. She commented, "When she walks out of that room, you will see a real Celtic princess."

A few moments later, the door opened and Emma Sinead walked out dressed in a beautiful two tone green dress with Celtic symbols on both sleeves, her necklace clearly visible. Both the doctor and Ellinor, lost for words, just sat and smiled.

"Grandmama, it is so beautiful!" Emma Sinead said, as she twirled round. "Mama, Papa, do you like it?"

Ellinor said, "You look stunning! Your grandmother was right, you look just like a princess."

"Papa?" asked Emma Sinead.

"What can I say?" Jose said, "you look amazing! And to think only a few months ago, you were just a child. We are all so proud of you."

Ellinor then spoke, "Now, princess, it's time for your bed and make sure you put the dress away properly."

Emma Sinead gave each of them a hug and a kiss and commented, "I thank God for such a lovely family and thank you, Grandmama for being my best grandmother."

"I think," Anabella remarked, "that I am your only grandmother." As Emma Sinead entered her room, she turned, smiled, and said, "You are the best grandmother anyone could have."

Ellinor looked to Jose and Anabella and said, "She has grown so much since we came here, she is almost like a different girl." A few moments later, Emma Sinead appeared again. "Mama, Maria sent me a message to say there is a big TV show in the school on Friday, but they don't know what it is. She thinks it's a movie."

Her mother answered, "Please don't tell her that you are the big star."

All three sat up talking well into the night.

Chapter 19

Eight o'clock next morning, as the Salvador family sat in the dining room having breakfast, Nadia entered the dining hall and walked straight to their table. "There has been a slight change of plan Ellinor, after breakfast you, Emma Sinead and Anabella will be coming with me. We are driving straight to Windsor. Miss Michelle Carter-Jones thinks it would be much better if Emma Sinead spends a little more time at the Castle. Shall we say thirty minutes?"

Ellinor answered, "Nadia, we are ready, we just need to fetch some things from our room." Ellinor turned to Jose, "What will you do, Jose? I have no idea what time we will return."

Before Jose could reply, the four girls appeared, with Isaac trotting beside Nikita.

"Nikita," Nadia spoke with a stern voice, "you know that Isaac is not allowed in the dining hall."

"Mother," Nikita replied. "He has just come in to wish Emma Sinead good luck. And he will leave immediately."

"Ok," Nadia said.

"I will take him to the reception area," said Emma Sinead, as she took hold of his lead, "let's go, Isaac!" they both left the dining room.

Anabella turned to Ellinor smiling, she said, "I don't think you need to worry about Jose, he has lots of great company. I'm sure the girls will look after him."

Nikita spoke, "We are waiting for father. Doctor Jose, has he told you we are flying to Carlisle and then to Scotland this morning?"

Everyone looked at Nikita in surprise. "No," replied Jose, "your father has not mentioned anything."

"I think he was so busy last evening he forgot," replied Nikita. Alex walked into the lounge. "Are we organised?" he asked.

"Father," said Nikita, "I have just told Doctor de Salvador where we are going."

"I am sorry Jose," said Alex, "I did not want to say anything until I was sure we were going. Will everyone be ready in 30 minutes please?"

"Can I ask why we are going to - what's the name again, Nikita?" enquired Jose.

"It's called Carlisle and is on the way to Scotland. From Carlisle, we travel to a village on the Scottish coast. We are going to see something in an old abbey."

Nine o'clock and everyone stood outside the hotel's main entrance, awaiting their transport to their respective destinations. Two cars arrived, the first driven by Caroline, a seven seat Ford Galaxy. Nadia decided it would be best if Anabella sat in the front passenger seat and herself, Ellinor and Emma Sinead behind. The second car, a Rolls Royce silver shadow. "Ok, ladies, Jose, we have a flight schedule to keep. Let's go!" Alex said.

Then Jose quickly walked over and gave his wife a kiss on the cheek and as he hugged Emma Sinead, he whispered, "I know you will be fine and you can tell me all about it this evening."

As they drove down the M23, Jose asked, "How long will the trip take?"

"I'm sorry Jose," replied Alex, "I forgot to tell you, we're flying to Carlisle from Gatwick, it's about one hour's flying time." The car turned on to the airport road, speeding past the main terminal building and stopping in front of a large hanger. A security guard greeted them. "Good morning, Mr Andrusanke, I believe your plane is fuelled and good to go."

"Thank you," replied Alex. The security guard greeted Nikita. "Good Morning, Miss Nikita, I hope you have a nice flight."

"We will, Robert," she replied, "the weather is excellent for flying." They entered the hanger, Jose looked in amazement to see a Lear jet in front of him. "Nikita," he asked, "are we travelling in this?"

"Doctor de Salvador," she replied, "this is father's toy."

"My God it's beautiful!" exclaimed the doctor, "and please call me Jose," he replied, as he climbed the short steps and stepped into the cabin. "Wow! I never realised they looked like this inside."

"If you are going to travel, Jose," replied Alex, "do it in style, and with a little comfort! Please Jose, sit here," he said, pointing to four seats with a table between. Nikita came in carrying a folder. "Father, I have the flight plans, but unfortunately we have a 30 minute wait."

"Jose," said Alex as he stood up, "let me introduce you to our pilot for this trip." Jose looked round.

"No, here is our pilot," Alex said indicating to his daughter Nikita.

Jose looked at Nikita, "You fly this? I cannot even manage a bicycle."

"But doctor, sorry Jose," Nikita replied, "I cannot perform heart surgery."

"Don't worry," answered Alex, "my daughter is one of the best pilots you can have." The door between cabin and the cockpit was open, Jose could see and hear Nikita talking to air traffic control. "I am so impressed with Nikita," Jose said. "I never imagined a young girl flying a complicated jet like this, wait until I tell Emma Sinead."

Alex laughed, "My dear friend, she may ask you to buy a plane for her!"

Flying over the midlands of England, Jose remarked, "I never imagined I would be sightseeing in England from this height."

Alex laughed, "Sometimes Jose it's the best way."

Soon they were landing at Carlisle airport, a helicopter already waiting for the short hop to Whitethorn, a small village on the west coast.

The helicopter landed in an open field next to the abbey. Father Ryan, the local priest, stood near the wooden gate by the entrance to the field, waiting to greet them. Alex introduced everyone.

"You said there were five girls, Mr Andrusanke?" Father Ryan said.

"The fifth girl could not make it today," Alex replied. "This is her father, Doctor Jose de Salvador, from Buenos Aries in Argentina. Due to another engagement, which you will hear all about over the next few days, his daughter, Emma Sinead could not travel with us."

"First, let me show you round the old Abbey," Father Ryan said as he walked briskly along the gravel path towards the old abbey, giving them a running commentary of its history as he walked. "The Abbey or Priory, as some people call it, was built by Saint Ninian in the year 397AD, on the site of an old Celtic settlement. Saint Ninian brought Christianity to the Celts. And even to this day, we still have Celtic ways within the Catholic Church, such as the festival of light which is Christmas and Celtic cross on modern gravestones."

As they got close to the ruined abbey, Father Ryan pointed out some of the features of the abbey which still had its four walls and sand stone arched entrance, but sadly no roof or doors. The priest stopped and explained how they got a government grant to repair the floor of the Abbey. "We decided to remove the large stone slabs and re-lay them on a concrete base. During this renovation the workmen discovered another floor underneath. You are standing on the old floor now." "Please," he said, pointing down to the floor, "look at the designs on the slabs." As they walked round, they could see, carved into the stone slabs, all the planets, the Sun being the centre. "Have you noticed?" said the priest, "they put the sun in the centre." He continued, "These were carved at least one thousand years before Galileo made his famous statement to the Christian church." He then pointed to a large flat stone in front of the Altar. "At first, we thought it was a grave, but when we removed the slab, a stone staircase was visible, leading to a medium-sized room." His tone of his voice now raised a little, "Inside the room, there was a stone altar with a Celtic cross carved into the wall." He continued in an excited voice, "And resting against the cross was a flat stone, about 300 cm square with carvings on it. I have never seen a carving like it in my life." Everyone listened intently to his description.

Afraid of missing their return time slot at Carlisle Alex spoke, "Where is the carving now, father?"

"I removed it for safe keeping, and placed it in our church. Let me take you there." They walked from the Abbey along the winding gravel path, and into the church. The priest walked in front towards the main altar and alongside a reinforced glass case, draped with a green cover which had Celtic symbols stitched with a golden thread. This reminded Jose of Emma Sinead's dress.

The priest removed the cover, folded it carefully and placed it to one side. Inside the glass case was a beautifully carved stone tablet, one edge looking as if it had been broken. The carved image depicted four tall girls. Each wearing a tiara, Celtic style dresses and holding out their hands as a greeting. One girl standing in front, held something in her hand as if she was presenting it to someone. Jose tried to see what she held in her hand. "It must be on the missing piece!" he exclaimed.

"What does the writing say?" asked Saya. The priest spoke, "It is a mixture of two languages, Latin and old Gaelic. But part is missing, I had a man come here from the British Museum to decipher the wording, it reads:

From the four corners of the globe, the four princesses came."

"Father," Nikita spoke, "each of the girls is wearing a necklace."

"I need a magnifying glass, it is too small for my eyes," he answered. The priest walked away and returned with a large magnifying glass. "Wait!" the priest said as he reached out to the glass case, I will open the top for you." Alex bent over, peering through the magnifying glass. There was silence. He spoke, "It is hard to believe that this stone carving is over 2000 years old."

The priest interrupted, "I have no words to describe the events that are happening. Could it be that something the ancients predicted is coming true?" He turned to Alex, "Tell me," he asked, "what is the fifth girl going to do? You said I would know soon."

"I am sorry, my friend," replied Alex, "I cannot tell you, but watch your television news over the next few days."

The priest turned to the girls, "I don't know if the stone was broken by accident?" he said.

Nikita answered, "Father Ryan it was broken to hide it's true meaning."

Alex spoke, "Father, I am afraid we have run out of time. We need to get back to the airport or we may lose our slot." As they walked back to the helicopter, the priest spoke, "Next Sunday's service will be a celebration. I will place the stone carving at the centre of the altar."

Nikita, alarmed, spoke sharply to the priest, "Father! You must not display the tablet."

He looked at Nikita, "Can you tell me why it cannot be displayed?" he asked.

Nikita answered, "For now it must remain hidden from prying eyes."

Alex thanked the priest for allowing them into his church and promised they would return with all five girls.

As they walked out of the church, Jose took the gold embossed case from his jacket, handed it to the priest and asked, "Father, can you tell me what this writing says?"

The priest held the case firmly, his hands began to tremble as he spoke in an excited voice, "*don chuigiu agus deiridh banphironsa*. It means for the fifth and final princess."

"Where did you get this, doctor?" asked the priest.

"It contained a necklace, which was a birthday gift to my daughter," he answered, as he boarded the helicopter.

Father Ryan handed the box back to Jose and whispered in his ear, "The prophesy is coming true." He turned and walked slowly back to his church, as he approached the altar he was sure he had seen a faint green glow coming from the glass case containing the stone carving, then placing the cover on the case he felt a great calm as if a weight had been lifted off his body.

Alex Andrusanke and his guests just made their slot at Carlisle airport and were soon airborne again, heading for Gatwick.

Jose sat with Alex and asked, "What did the priest mean when he whispered to me the prophesy is coming true?"

Alex looked at Jose and was not sure how to answer the question without alarming him, he thought for a moment and said, "I suppose you could say the Celts are just like the Jews, who are still waiting for the messiah, the Celts are waiting for the fifth princess."

Alex was thankful the conversation was interrupted by Nikita announcing their arrival at Gatwick Airport.

On the way back to Brighton Alex spoke, "Jose, on Sunday morning we will all be travelling to Ireland. But now I think we might try to do a little detour."

"You mean back to Whitethorn?" Jose asked.

Alex replied, "Jose, did you see the look on the priest's face when he saw the girls? He recognised a connection to the tablet immediately."

Chapter 20

Back at the Hotel, Emma Sinead, sitting in the lounge with her mother, grandmother and Nadia was all excited waiting for her father to return. Nadia received a call from Alex to say they were just driving into Brighton. The four girls could be heard before anyone appeared. They were the first to enter the lounge followed by Jose and Alex.

Emma Sinead rushed over, "Papa, I am so happy to see you, I have lots to tell you!"

"Well!" replied her father, "should you not have greeted everyone first?"

"I am so sorry, Papa." She gave Alex a kiss on the cheek and embraced the girls. They all sat down in the dining hall for a late evening meal, and listened to Emma Sinead's story of the day's events at Windsor Castle.

Alex spoke, "Tomorrow is going to be a busy day and an early start, I suggest we all have an early night."

Just after Emma Sinead went to bed, Jose sat in the kitchen with Ellinor and Anabella. He explained the surprise trip to Carlisle, and the helicopter trip to Whitethorn in Scotland. He spoke softly, "An old ruined Abbey and a little church lay just outside the village. The local priest took us first to the old Abbey. He told us that when the builders were repairing the old floor, they discovered a room underneath where the altar used to be, the room he said, had been covered for over two thousand years! The priest then took us to the small church alongside the Abbey, and beside the altar was a large glass case. He removed the green covering, and pointed to the object inside." Jose handed some photographs to Ellinor, who studied them carefully. "Is this true? This stone is more than two thousand years old!"

"Yes," Jose replied. "Look carefully at the figures in the carving."

"This is not possible!" gasped Ellinor. "Look, one girl is holding her hands as if she is handing something to someone else and they are all tall like the four girls." She handed the photograph to her mother. "It's a pity the piece is missing," Anabella remarked. Jose then handed Ellinor two more photographs, which had better definition. "The girls are all wearing tiaras and necklaces. My God! The necklace looks identical to Emma Sinead's" she exclaimed. "What does the writing say? Does anyone know?" Ellinor asked.

Jose produced a sheet of paper with the translation and handed it to Anabella. He said, "The language is a mixture of old Gaelic and Latin."

Anabella read the words aloud. "From the four corners of the globe, the four princesses came."

"Was that carved into the stone two thousand years ago?" Ellinor asked. She looked to Anabella. "Mother! Is there a connection to the girls and Emma Sinead? And why was it broken?" Before Anabella could answer Jose spoke, "I heard Nikita telling the priest it was broken to hide its true meaning."

Anabella spoke, "Your grandfather used to say that the Irish Celts have fairies working for them who know everything of the past, present and the future."

"I wish we could talk to one now," muttered Ellinor.

"They are telling us in stone," replied Anabella.

Jose spoke, "The priest said that the three figures are holding their hands out in the sign of greeting, and the fourth figure is presenting something, she is holding out her hand to someone else, but until we find the other half, we will never know." Jose continued, "I am sure the missing figure will be the fifth Princess!" He then took the box that held Emma Sinead's necklace from his jacket. He placed it on the table, "When the priest held this, his hand was trembling. He translated the writing and told me it reads, For the fifth and final princess."

Ellinor spoke in a soft voice, "No matter what we say or do, Emma Sinead's life is being guided by a force we know nothing about."

Anabella spoke, "She is being guided by her great-grandfather and he is protecting her."

Jose spoke, "We are travelling to Ireland next Sunday, but I think we will be travelling via Scotland. Alex thinks it's right for the Scottish priest to meet with Emma Sinead."

Ellinor yawned, "We have a busy and very important day tomorrow, we should all go to bed and have a good night's sleep."

Chapter 21

Alex and Nadia were already in the dining hall when the others arrived.

Nikita walked directly to where her father was sitting, and in a low voice she spoke, "Father, I need to talk with you."

"This sounds important, let's go quickly to my office." Before her father could close the office door, Nikita said, "Father we must return to St Ninians Abbey, it's very important." Her father answered, "I had already decided to fly to Scotland first and then on to Ireland, but hadn't made any plans. I'll ask Caroline to organise everything for Sunday."

"Thank you," Nikita answered, "you're such an understanding father."

"Ok, let's return to the dining hall," Alex said.

Every guest at the Belmont Hotel realised something was happening when a gleaming white Rolls Royce appeared outside. The car, bearing the flags of the United Kingdom and Argentina. Three police motorcyclists had parked opposite the Hotel. The Argentinean ambassador and his wife stepped out and walked through the entrance of the hotel. By this time, the police had already begun the task of diverting traffic off the main road. A few moments later, and with precision timing, the Salvador family, the Argentinean ambassador and his wife walked briskly from the hotel to the waiting car and left immediately.

Following in a dark blue Rolls Royce, was Alex, Nadia, Anabella and Mr Michael Hagen from the foreign office. They were soon joined by a third car, a silver Mercedes driven by a member of the foreign office team with the four girls. The three cars entered the main traffic heading towards the M23 accompanied by a police escort.

At precisely ten minutes past twelve, they arrived at the gates to Windsor Castle. The three cars drove straight through and stopped outside the great hall. As they walked towards the entrance of the hall, they were met by Michelle Carter-Jones who escorted them through the building to the reception hall. There were 6 rows of seats facing a central area, each seat having a name tag attached. The Salvador family and the Ambassadors group were escorted to the front row. Emma Sinead sitting between her mother and father with the Ambassador and his wife sitting next to her father, and Michael Hagen beside her mother.

The ambassador spoke, "Are you a little nervous, Emma Sinead?"

"No sir," she answered. "But I think Mama is." There was a lot of noise coming from behind and Emma Sinead wanted so much to look round, but she held her composure and just looked ahead. Miss Michelle Carter-Jones walked over and handed Emma Sinead a small bunch of flowers, which had arrived that morning on a flight from Buenos Aries, "These are for you to present to her Majesty Queen Elizabeth."

At precisely twelve thirty, the side door opened and a voice said, "Please rise for Her Majesty, Queen Elizabeth." The Queen entered, followed by the Duke of Edinburgh. As she approached, she stopped and talked with Mr Michael Hagen, who introduced the Queen to the Argentinean Ambassador and his wife. Stepping forward, Michael spoke, "Your Majesty, it gives me great pleasure to introduce Miss Emma Sinead de Salvador from Buenos Aries, Argentina." Emma Sinead gave a graceful curtsey. She handed the flowers to the Queen, and in a quiet but strong voice said, "Your Majesty, on behalf of the government and people of Argentina, I present this gift to you."

"What lovely flowers!" The Queen answered, "have they come all the way from Argentina?"

"Yes m'am," Emma Sinead answered.

The Queen then surprised her. "I hear you were a little nervous and were not sure whether I would speak in Spanish or English." Then speaking in perfect Spanish: *"Es un honour dar la bienbenida a usted ya su familia al Reino Unido y al Castillo de Windsor y espero un dia para poder visitarlo en su pais."* Emma Sinead smiled, and thanked the Queen in Spanish.

The Queen moved on, and talked briefly with Emma Sinead's mother and father. "Doctor and Mrs de Salvador, you are so fortunate to have a lovely daughter like Emma Sinead and I do hope, one day, to be able to visit you in your country." Her Majesty then walked over and talked with Emma Sinead's grandmother and to Mr And Mrs Andrusanke, she thanked

Alex Andrusanke for all the work he has done for the United Kingdom. She turned, walked over and talked briefly with the four girls.

Meantime the Duke of Edinburgh was talking and joking with Emma Sinead. He remarked, "I believe it was your 13th birthday a few days ago, and you received a beautiful gift."

"Yes I did Sir," she replied. The Duke commented, "Emma Sinead, you are a credit to your country and maybe one day we will meet again, but next time in Buenos Aries."

"I hope so sir," she replied. Emma Sinead was now more aware of all the clicking cameras in the room and it was only as she turned round to leave the hall, that she saw the full extent of the media.

Before they left the castle, there was the customary photo shoot and a brief talk with the press.

As they made their way to their cars, Nadia asked Ellinor, "Did you imagine anything like this, when you first planned your trip to the United Kingdom?"

Ellinor exclaimed, "My God! Had I known this was going to happen, I would never have come!"

"But now it's over, you are glad you came?"

"Yes," Ellinor replied. "It was an unbelievable experience for myself and Jose, but how Emma Sinead coped, I will never know." As the motorcade made its way back to the Belmont Hotel, Emma Sinead whispered to her mother, "Did I do everything correctly?" Ellinor put her arm round the shoulder of her daughter. "Your father and I are so proud! A few days ago, you were a 12-year-old child and now you are grown up. But I am a little worried, as to what will happen on our return. I mean, with your school."

"Mama," Emma Sinead responded, "you forget, I am a Salvador and O'Houlihan. We can adapt to any quest!" Her mother, stunned by the reply, laughed, "Yes, you are a Salvador and an O'Houlihan!"

As the three cars approached the Belmont Hotel, Alex received a call informing him that there were groups of reporters outside the main entrance. He contacted the Ambassador and instructed him to follow his car. As the cars pulled into the drive of Nikita's house, the Ambassador decided that he would drop off his guests and carry on to his residence in

London.

Alex Andrusanke spoke to the five girls, "It would be best if we all use the underground entrance to the hotel and Michael Hagen will inform the press and tell them that a press release will be issued by the Foreign Office shortly." A special dinner had been arranged in the Belmont to celebrate the event.

Chapter 22

The head teacher of Emma Sinead's school in Buenos Aries, made an announcement to the pupils who had assembled in the main hall for registration.

"This morning, we had a visit from the Educational Minister, who told me that something of importance is going to take place tomorrow late afternoon in the United Kingdom, and it involves our school. A large television screen is to be positioned in the assembly hall, and this afternoon, each of you will receive a letter inviting your parents to attend. The letter you receive will contain all the details. I am sorry, I cannot tell you more, the truth is that I do not know any more."

The next day the school was alive with excitement. The assembly hall was now fitted out with new seats, the parquet flooring cleaned and polished. By 15:00 the assembly hall was full. The Minister of Education stood on the stage and spoke, "A Meeting is about to take place in the United Kingdom between two special people, and in a few moments, you children will see how your school is involved." Suddenly the large screen came to life.

It began with an aerial view of London, and quickly moved to Windsor Castle. The commentators speaking in Spanish. The schoolchildren watched the TV screen in silence, as a white Rolls Royce bearing the flags of both countries arrived at the entrance to Windsor Castle. The silence suddenly erupted into cheers when they saw Emma Sinead step out of the car. "It's Emma Sinead!" The children shouted and clapped. Maria Fernandez, Emma Sinead's friend, was so surprised, she could not believe she was seeing her best friend meet the Queen of England!

The following Monday at school assembly, the head teacher spoke, "Friday was a special day for our school." He held up some newspapers. One headline had a full front-page photograph of Emma Sinead, smiling and talking to the Queen. The heading read, "The Dove of Peace flies from Argentina to Great Britain." He continued, "To represent your country is a great honour. I am so proud that a pupil from our school has done just that."

Later that day, a large framed photograph of the Queen of England being greeted by Emma Sinead was hung in the school reception area.

Chapter 23

At first light, two cars made their way through the private, high-security gates of Gatwick Airport and drove straight to Mr Andrusanke's Lear jet 25. Michael Hagen was already standing by the plane. "Glad you could make it," said Alex, "Nadia told me you're also coming to Ireland."

"I don't seem to have any choice, if I'm to find out what the big mystery is."

As the flight would be leaving the United Kingdom's airspace, security and immigration checks would be necessary. When they were about to board the plane, Emma Sinead noticed Nikita and her father walking towards an office building. She nudged her father, "Papa, is Nikita not coming with us today?"

"I hope so," replied her father, "Nikita is the pilot and she has to file a flight plan." Emma Sinead looked astonished. "Nikita is going to fly this big plane?"

"Don't worry dear," replied her father, "Nikita can fly this better than I drive my car." Just then, a young trainee immigration officer came over. "Excuse me sir, may I ask your daughter for her autograph?"

"Of course you can!" replied Jose. The young man produced a piece of paper and a pen. "I saw you on the television last Friday talking with the Queen. Could you sign your autograph for me?" He held out the piece of paper and pen, and as Emma Sinead took the pen and paper, she turned to her father, "Papa, what should I write?"

"Well," her father said, "first you ask him his name," blushing slightly, she turned to the young man and asked, "may I have your name please?"

"My name is John," he replied. Her father turned to her and said, "Now just write 'To John, best wishes, Emma Sinead de Salvador'." The young man, by now blushing bright red, thanked her and walked away. Emma

Sinead, still slightly red in the face, walked up the short steps and into the plane. Her mother looked at her husband and smiled.

As the plane travelled down the runway, Emma Sinead listened intently to the chatter between the control tower and Nikita, then she heard the word 'rotate.' "What does rotate mean, Papa?" she asked. "I think it means you have enough speed to take off," he replied. The forty-five minute flight was uneventful and they were soon landing at Carlisle Airport. A quick car journey across the small airport to two waiting military helicopters, which had been organised by Michael Hagen. They boarded quickly and were soon on their way to the village of Whitethorn.

Ten thirty, the church attached to the old Abbey in Whitethorn was full. Which meant no more than about thirty-five people, and all of them looking for more information. The village was rife with rumours, and they needed answers about the mysterious stone sculptor and the four girls who had now been christened, 'The Princesses of Whitethorn.'

The priest had just finished his service and walked slowly to the pulpit. He stood there in silence for a few moments, then spoke, "If you want answers, I do not have any. The strange events that have taken place over the past few days, of which you are all aware, makes me think there is a strong connection between our stone carving and the four girls. It has been suggested by the girls, the stone tablet should remain hidden and so for now, it will remain covered over." Before he could continue, there was a loud noise of engines passing overhead, and then silence. The priest waited for a moment, "I am sorry about that," he said, "I think they are rescue helicopters returning to base." He was about to continue, when the large wooden door at the entrance to the church opened.

First in the door was Emma Sinead, followed by the four girls and they walked slowly towards the altar. Alex Andrusanke, his wife and the rest of the group stood just inside the door. Each of the five girls acknowledged the priest with a slight bow as they walked past the pulpit. They stood in front of the altar, facing the now covered stone tablet. Emma Sinead reached out and slowly removed the cover. Carefully folding it and placing it to one side, she placed her hand on the tablet. A deathly silence descended on the congregation. Without warning an eerie green glow emanated from the tablet, and within minutes had penetrated every corner of the church. The priest mesmerised by the events taking place, walked slowly from the pulpit and stood facing the altar.

The five girls turned and faced the small congregation. Nikita intoned,

"Many centuries have passed, and now it has come full circle. We are united." Then looking to Emma Sinead she continued, "This is Emma Sinead de Salvador, soon to be the fifth Celtic Princess." The congregation, now bathed in a green glow, stood in silence as if hypnotised. Alex and the rest of the group still waiting at the main entrance. The priest beckoned them forward and they walked slowly down the narrow aisle. Alex walked over to the priest and whispered, "I am sorry not to have given you some notice of our return, I had to organise everything so quickly."

Anabella went straight to Emma Sinead and put her arms round her, and with tears in her eyes said, "Every word that your great-grandfather told me, is coming true."

Emma Sinead then presented her family to the priest and the small congregation. She whispered in her grandmother's ear, "Grandmama! The stone tablet must be returned to Ireland to be joined."

"You have to do this today?" she asked.

"Yes, it must be done now!" Emma Sinead replied.

Anabella turned to Alex, "Emma Sinead has said that she must take the stone tablet to Ireland and will return it intact and complete." Alex explained to Father Ryan what needed to be done.

Without question, Father Ryan walked to the altar, carefully picking up the stone tablet, he presented it to Emma Sinead. As it was heavy, Alex took charge and carried it out to one of the waiting helicopters.

Emma Sinead then turned to the priest, "Padre, sorry, Father, could you please take me to the secret room?"

"Please follow me," he answered and turning to his congregation, he said "please wait here." Emma Sinead and the four girls followed the priest.

Ellinor looked worried. "Where are they going?" she asked. "And how did Emma Sinead know about this secret room?"

"Ellinor, in time you will know everything, she wants to visit the Abbey and the secret room," answered Anabella. The priest walked briskly along the gravel path towards the old Abbey, followed closely by the five girls, their family and the villagers, who were not prepared to miss out on whatever was about to happen.

As they entered the Abbey, Father Ryan was surprised to see that the heavy stone slab was no longer covering the secret room, the entrance and staircase were now clearly visible. This surprised him. The stone, weighing several tons, had been in place for over three months and was in place when he visited the Abbey that very morning.

The four girls stood at the entrance, while Emma Sinead walked slowly down the stone steps. Anabella held her daughter's hand and said, "Don't worry Ellinor, Emma Sinead will be fine. Her great-grandfather is holding her hand." As in the church, an eerie green glow seemed to pour out of the underground room as if it were liquid.

A young, 8-year-old girl in the congregation, squeezed her mother's hand. "Look, mother! the necklaces on the four girls are shining brightly." Everyone looked at the girls, who were standing motionless round the entrance. The necklaces were indeed shining brightly and pulsating. After a short time, Emma Sinead re-appeared, and as she reached the entrance of the room, her mother felt sure that she was little taller. The priest just stared in silence.

Emma Sinead walked straight over to the villagers and took the hand of the young girl. She whispered in her ear, "Now, you will get better." Then turning to Alex and the priest said, "The quest has begun, the prophecy can now be completed."

All too soon, the visit was over. The five girls were leaving again, to return to Carlisle Airport and head across the Irish Sea to Shannon Airport. The priest and the parishioners returned to the church. He spoke to his small congregation, "I still have no answers for what has just happened, you have seen it all, just like me."

As the sound of the helicopters faded in the distance, the priest turned to the young girl and asked, "What did she whisper to you?" The young girl, who was receiving treatment for a rare cancer, looked at her mother and said, "When she held my hand mother, it was like a fire! And she told me I will get better."

"She said that to you?" her mother asked.

"Yes, mother," she answered. The mother, Mrs McBride, looked at the priest. "Father Ryan, how did she know my daughter was ill?"

One week later, the young girl and her mother sat in the waiting room of Carlisle Hospital, for another scan and more blood tests. The doctor approached, "And how are you today, young lady?" he asked.

The young girl answered, "I feel much better today, doctor." The doctor looked at her and said, "You know when we last met, I told you there would be some good days and some bad days."

"I know that doctor, but now every day is good and today I feel so good."

"Well," replied the doctor, "let's see what the test results tell us." While the young girl was having her scan, the doctor spoke to her mother. "Mrs McBride, we have done everything medically possible to stop the spread of the cancer. There is nothing more we can do, we have tried everything to slow it down, everything we try is only more trauma for your daughter and all to no avail. It is with deep regret, I can only tell you that your daughter will have no more than two months at the most." Mrs McBride looked at the doctor, smiled and said, "Let's wait and see what the Good Lord has in store for us."

The doctor, a little surprised by her candid remark could only say, "Let's wait and see Mrs McBride."

After Mrs McBride and her daughter had left the hospital the doctor spoke to the ward nurse, "I am worried the young girl's mother seems to be in a state of disbelief as to the seriousness of her daughter's condition."

As Mrs McBride and her daughter made their way home, the doctor's words played on her mind, and thinking about what Emma Sinead had whispered to her daughter, she asked "Are you really feeling better?" The young girl replied, "Mother, I feel very well, but it's not like before, now every day is good."

A few days later, a letter arrived from the hospital and fearing the worst, Mrs McBride waited for her husband to come home. As he entered the house, she handed him the letter. "You've not opened it," he said.

"No," she replied, "I didn't want to read it while I was alone."

He carefully opened the letter and read it slowly. He looked at his wife who was sitting at the table, both her hands covering her face. He spoke in an excited voice. "She is clear! No cancer, nothing! Her blood tests are good, and nothing on the scan." The next morning, the husband decided to go into work late, giving him time to contact the hospital. He got through immediately to reception, and asked to speak with someone on his daughter's old ward. The nurse on the ward confirmed the contents of the letter and explained that in some rare cancer cases this happens. She continued, "Mr McBride, your daughter's scans are all clear of any cancer. We would like to see her again in six months, simply for a normal check-up."

He turned to his wife, "It's true, she is cured. She is going to be ok."

News quickly spread round the village, and one by one the villagers walked to the church. Father Ryan sat in the sacristy preparing his sermon for the following Sunday. On hearing the noise coming from the church he peered out, but paid no attention, it was normal for villagers to come to the church from time to time, but then realising almost all the villagers were there, he knew something had happened.

As Father Ryan walked from his sacristy to investigate, Mrs McBride entered the church, she walked straight to the altar and with both her arms outstretched she said out loud, "Thank you, whoever you are."

The priest, fearing the worst, walked over quickly to her side. "Is it your daughter?" he asked. She produced the letter from the hospital and handed it to him. After carefully reading its content, he commented, "This is the best news I have had in a long time!" Mrs McBride turned towards the villagers. "The hospital confirmed the letter on the telephone just thirty minutes ago." The villagers stood facing the altar and all made the sign of the cross.

The priest spoke, "As I have repeated many times to all of you and you Mrs McBride, I have no answers for what we witnessed on Sunday, but only good can come of it. I now implore all of you, to keep silent about all the events that have taken place. We do not want our village or church to turn into some magical place, we are in the safe hands of the five princesses."

Mrs McBride answered, "Father, nothing more will be said. I am truly thankful for the life of our daughter."

Chapter 24

The helicopter flight from Whitethorn lasted no more than 45 minutes. After landing at Carlisle Airport they wasted no time in boarding the Lear jet for their short flight to Shannon Airport.

As the plane sped down the runway, Emma Sinead spoke to her grandmother in a soft voice, "Grandmama, do you think Mr Andrusanke is very rich to own a plane like this?"

"Maybe so, but look at how hard he works," replied her grandmother. "Papa!" Emma Sinead called out loudly, "can you buy a plane like this?"

"Sure," he replied, as he laughed, "I'll order one when we return home. Which colour would you like?"

Alex came in from the flight deck. "Just to let you know, we will be arriving at Shannon Airport in fifty-five minutes," and turning to Emma Sinead, "would you like to go and sit with Nikita?"

"Could I?" she asked excitedly. "Yes, you can," Alex answered, "but just before landing, you must return to your seat." Emma Sinead did not need a second chance offer, as she sat in the cockpit, thinking, "If only my friends in school could see me now."

Just then, Alex returned with Emma Sinead's Ipad, pointed it and took a photograph saying, "Now you can send that to your friends."

During the flight, Nikita explained some of the controls and showed her how the plane could fly on automatic pilot.

Alex sat with Michael Hagen, "Do I need to explain what you have just witnessed at the Abbey?" Alex asked.

"Alex, what I have seen should be reported to my government. But it would be masses of paperwork and in the end, who would believe it? I am sure they will find out soon enough."

The journey had no sooner started and were soon flying over Ireland, the fifty-five minute flight went by quickly. Alex announced that they were approaching Shannon, and asked Emma Sinead to return her seat and put her seat belt on.

The plane taxied to a private hanger and parked up. As the door of the plane opened, Customs and Immigration officers came inside.

"Good Morning, Mr Andrusanke. Lovely to see you again, and of course, Michael Hagen who we have not seen for a number of years."

"It's always good to be back in Ireland," Michael replied. One of the officers walked through the plane carrying a folded newspaper in his hand. He paused in front of Emma Sinead, and said in a soft voice, "We won't have any problems recognising this beautiful girl!" as he unfolded the newspaper, The Irish Independent. On its front page, a large photograph of Emma Sinead with the headlines, "The dove of peace hits the hearts of two nations."

He quickly checked the passports of the Salvador family and Saya Akira. As he looked at Saya's passport he asked, "Are you still climbing mountains, Miss Akira?"

"Yes, I'm afraid so," she replied. He then turned to one of his colleagues. "This girl climbs mountains without even a rope for security."

"I know," replied his colleague, "I have seen her on television." He looked at her and said, "Miss Akira, you are either crazy or brave." Saya laughed, "maybe I'm crazy," she replied. "Well! Miss, I think you are brave."

"Thank you," she said. Emma Sinead turned and asked Saya, "Do you really climb mountains?"

"Yes," she replied. "It's my hobby."

"Are they like hills or big mountains?" Emma Sinead asked.

"Some are big and some are just like big rocks. I'll show you some photographs when we get to the hotel."

Emma Sinead turned to her mother, "Mama, are you nervous about meeting our relatives?"

"I suppose a little," she continued, "no, not nervous, just a little apprehensive."

"Grandmama, are you nervous to meet our relatives?" Emma Sinead asked. Anabella replied, "No, I am not nervous, I don't think they will eat us."

"Mrs Fernandez, don't be too sure about that," replied one of the immigration officers with a smile.

"Mr Andrusanke, everything is in order here," said the officer, as he handed the stamped passports back to their respective owners. "Could I suggest you take your party through the main terminal, the press have got hold of information that this little lady, pointing to Emma Sinead, is visiting relatives in Ireland."

"I see no reason not to do that," replied Alex. "What do you think Jose?"

"That's ok," replied Jose, "providing they remember she is only thirteen-years-old and not too many questions." As they left the plane, Emma Sinead asked, "Nikita, is it difficult to fly a plane?"

"Once you know how, it's easy, but you have to learn a lot and study hard," Nikita replied. "Maybe one day I will learn," Emma Sinead answered.

"I hope so, Emma Sinead," Nikita said.

The party boarded the airport shuttle for the short journey to the main terminal and entered through a side door, the immigration officer leading them, as they walked directly to a small room which was full of reporters. Ellinor de Salvador held her husband's hand and asked, "are they all here just to see Emma Sinead?"

"I think so," he replied. They spent about thirty minutes answering questions and having photographs taken. Then Alex decided it was time to go. "Ladies and gentlemen, I am sorry, but we have a busy day ahead of us. Thank you very much."

Alex then escorted his group out to the main building. As they walked through the outer doors, there was applause and shouts of, "Welcome to Ireland Emma Sinead!"

It was a little too much for the 13-year-old Argentinean girl. She grabbed her mother's hand and squeezed it tight. Her mother looked at her and said, "Can you imagine what it will be like when we return to Buenos Aries?" As it was Sunday, Emma Sinead's photo appeared in the front page of every Irish Newspaper, which resulted in a large crowd of children inside and outside the terminal building. Two Garda officers made a pathway through the crowds and children with their parents had congregated round the cars. "Emma!" they called out, "can we have your autograph?" as they thrust pieces of paper in front of her. "Mama, what should I do?" she asked. "Well," her mother replied, "you cannot disappoint children!" as she handed Emma Sinead a pen. She signed her name on all kinds of scraps of paper. "Now you know what a pop star feels like!" her father remarked.

As Emma Sinead got in the car, a nun approached her, and in Spanish said, "Miss, I come from Buenos Aries, you are an angel."

That remark made Emma Sinead smile. "Thank you," replied Ellinor. "Thank you."

Alex got into the passenger side of the first car and directed the driver to go. Jose, Ellinor and Nadia sat directly behind, with Emma Sinead and Andrea who were both chatting in Spanish and laughing, in the back. The three girls, Anabella and Michael Hagen followed in the second car.

"Why is this country so green?" asked Jose. "Plenty of rain!" replied Alex. "But today is beautiful," exclaimed Jose. "I think," said Alex, glancing over his shoulder, "this year is an exception, a lot of good days. Also, I am sure God makes it rain when everyone is sleeping."

"Perfect organisation!" joked Jose.

Alex had arranged for everyone to stay at the famous Bunratty Castle hotel. As the cars pulled in, Jose asked, "Is this one of your Hotels, Alex?"

"No, I'm afraid not," Alex laughed. "They would not sell it to me, though I know the owner well, and we will have a good relaxing day." He continued, "They have a marvellous swimming pool, sauna, gym and a good size bar."

"Can I go swimming in the pool?" asked Emma Sinead. "Not right now," replied her mother. "We will go to our room first."

As they entered the hotel, Jose liked what he saw. The décor was just like the hotel in Brighton, with a large reception area. "This is beautiful!" remarked Ellinor.

"We always stay here every time we come to Ireland," Nadia answered, "but I think this is the first time for all four girls."

"Maybe the last time if they are noisy," laughed Alex.

"Good Morning, my dear friend from Russia!" A voice boomed out. "Patrick Ahern, my good friend!" Alex gave him the Russian bear hug. "Don't squeeze me too tight," Patrick remarked, "I am getting soft in my old age."

"Patrick, let me introduce you to my guests, but first, my daughter

Nikita." Patrick said to her, "Nikita, it's a great pleasure to meet you." As he took her hand, Nikita replied, "I am pleased to finally meet you. I know from mother and father, every time they are here, they love it." Patrick answered her, "Nikita, may I say you have your mother's looks but your father's height."

"Thank you," she replied. "You see, Alex," said Nadia, "everyone agrees that the looks come from the mother!"

"Patrick, let me introduce you to three more beautiful girls. They are my daughter's friends. Saya Akira from Tokyo, Andrea de Silva from Spain and Alessia Del Amato from Sorrento in Italy." Patrick smiled, "It's not every day i'm introduced to so many beautiful girls."

Then, just as Alex was about to introduce the Salvador family, Patrick Ahern spoke. "Well! It's not difficult to know who all of you are, especially this beautiful lady," pointing to Emma Sinead. "Your photograph, Emma Sinead, is in every newspaper, worldwide." Patrick continued, "Mrs de Salvador, Doctor de Salvador and Anabella Fernandez, welcome to The Bunratty Hotel."

Turning again to Emma Sinead, he said, "I am sure Miss Emma Sinead, the people of Ireland will welcome you into their hearts." Emma Sinead thanked him and gave a big smile.

Patrick gave her a kiss on the cheek and said, "Normally, we would greet you with a pint of Guinness, but for now, just a kiss." Emma Sinead looked quizzically at her mother, "What is Guinness, Mama?"

Her father told her, "It is a black beer especially made in Ireland and is not for young ladies!"

Patrick asked, "Would you like to have lunch first, or go straight to your rooms to freshen up?"

Alex answered, "I think everyone are going to their rooms first, you and I, Patrick, have some business to discuss." He continued, "It's now one-o-clock, let's all come down for a snack at say, two thirty."

Patrick reminded them, "We can do the paperwork when you return, just make sure you have your passports, they will be required." Just as they walked away, Nikita asked Patrick Ahern, "Is the swimming pool open today?"

"Yes it is," he replied.

Andrea interrupted, "Is the water warm, Mr Ahern?"

"My God! Miss, here in Ireland, we are all so tough we put ice in the pool!" he answered. "You put ice in the swimming pool?" Emma Sinead asked incredulously.

"That's ok then," replied Andrea with a laugh, "we can swim between the blocks of ice!"

"Just for you girls, the water will be a warm, twenty degrees." Patrick answered, as he smiled and walked away with Alex.

Chapter 25

Jose and family went to their room and Emma Sinead was quick to explore the two-bedroom apartment.

"Mama," Emma Sinead asked her mother, "could I share with Andrea? After all, she is in a room on her own."

"Don't you think you should ask Andrea first? Maybe her room is too small," her mother answered.

"Can I ring her?" asked Emma Sinead. "How do I find her number, Mama?"

"Have a look at the list by the telephone," her mother answered, "I think you dial zero for reception then ask for Andrea's room."

As Jose and Ellinor put their clothes in the wardrobe, they could hear Emma Sinead on the phone. "Excuse me, could you please connect me to Miss Andrea de Silva? I don't have her room number."

"Its room 223," replied the receptionist. "I will connect you now, but next time just dial 9 and then 223."

"Thank you," replied Emma Sinead. She then changed to Spanish as Andrea answered. "Hola Andrea, would you like me to share your room? Mama said I could, that is of course if you wish."

"That would be great," replied Andrea, "I am on the second floor, what's your room number?"

"Wait a moment please," Emma Sinead then called out to her mother, "Mama, what is our room number please?"

"It is room 402, that is on the fourth floor," her mother replied.

"Andrea, we are in room 402, on the fourth floor," Emma Sinead said.

"Ok," Andrea replied, "I will come and fetch you." A few minutes later and Andrea was at the door. "Remember girls! Reception at two thirty,"

Ellinor called out, "I will ring to remind you both."

"Ok Mama," replied Emma Sinead. "Wow!" remarked Jose, "silence is golden, but I would not be without her."

"Would you like coffee, my dear?" Ellinor asked, "Yes please!" was the reply.

Just then, the phone rang and Ellinor picked it up, "Mrs de Salvador, this is the receptionist. There is a Mr O'Houlihan on the line, asking to speak to you. Would you like me to put the call through?"

"Yes of course, put him through," she answered. "Hello," the voice at the other end said, "hello, is that Mrs de Salvador?"

"Yes it is," she replied.

"Mrs de Salvador," It's Peter O'Houlihan from Nenagh."

"Hello, Mr O'Houlihan, this is a surprise. How did you know we were here?" Peter O'Houlihan said to her, "Mrs de Salvador, that sounds very formal for cousins. Please, call me Peter, and may I call you by your first name?"

"Why yes, of course that's fine," replied Ellinor.

"Ellinor, we have tracked you, and your family through the television and newspapers. And on the radio this morning, they said you, and your family were in the Bunratty Castle hotel. I know Alex very well, he and I do a lot of business together. I would like to get as many of your cousins as possible, to meet with you, and your family when you come to Nenagh. Do you know when you will arrive here?"

"I have no idea Mr O'Houlihan, sorry, Peter, we are in the hands of Mr Alex Andrusanke."

"Ok Ellinor, don't worry, I will give Alex a ring and find out what his plans are."

"Yes, I think that is a good idea," she answered.

"I will do that right now," Peter replied.

"Ellinor, I look forward to meeting with you and your family. Goodbye for now, and as they say in Ireland, *slainte*."

Ellinor turned to her husband, "That was Peter O'Houlihan on the phone. He sounds like a nice person, I didn't imagine we would be meeting some of our relatives so soon."

Meanwhile, in room 223, Andrea and Emma Sinead were busy

exchanging information about their lives. "You sing beautifully," Emma Sinead said.

Andrea replied, "I love to sing songs that I write. I spend as much time as I can playing the piano and guitar."

"I like to play the pan pipes and flute," said Emma Sinead. "Recently, I read on the internet about a flute in Ireland they call the penny whistle and now I will learn to play that, but I am not good at singing," responded Emma Sinead. Andrea replied, "Maybe we can play some music together one day, and get our music on the radio. Also, do you know that Nikita and Alessia play the violin?"

"Does Saya play a musical instrument?" asked Emma Sinead.

"Saya, she is funny," replied Andrea, "she likes to play those big Japanese drums. You know those, they are huge drums and they go bom! bom! bom!"

"I cannot say I know them," replied Emma Sinead, "but if I saw one I might know it."

The two girls talked for hours. Andrea was very careful not to ask too many questions, or say too much that might worry Emma Sinead. So, she kept the conversation very low-key. Suddenly the phone rang. Andrea picked it up, "Hola?" It was Mrs de Salvador, and she spoke in Spanish, "*ok vamos a llegar allí, es su madre que tiene que ir a su habitación ahora.*"

Both girls made their way to room 402. When they entered, Ellinor told them, "It is nearly two thirty, time to go down to lunch!"

Jose came into the room, "Papa," Emma Sinead asked, "do you know what a big Japanese drum looks like?"

"Yes my dear, they are big, and heavy and are called Taiko drums. You have to be very strong and fit to play them."

"Papa, Saya plays them, Alessia and Nikita play the violin."

"Well, Emma Sinead, you play the pan pipes and the flute," before he could continue, Emma Sinead interrupted, "Papa, it's called a penny whistle here in Ireland."

"I am so sorry my dear, can you ever forgive me?" he laughed and continued, "maybe you girls should all get together and start a rock band."

"Papa, you cannot have a rock band with pan pipes and penny whistle," she scolded. Jose laughed, "Only joking, my darling."

111

Ellinor turned to her husband, "Jose, you must talk with Alex regarding our costs for the trip and for this hotel."

"I will do that today," he replied, "In fact, after lunch."

They made their way down to the reception area and walked into the huge dining hall, which was lined with tables. Each table full of food and standing behind each table, a chef and assistants.

"Mama, Papa," Emma Sinead said happily, "look at all the food! And there is even food from Argentina." Patrick Ahern approached them, "You are very fortunate! Today, we are sponsoring a World Food Day. Please visit all the tables and sample food from each country." Jose and Ellinor headed to the Argentinean table, and were busy chatting to the chef and his assistants, when Emma Sinead came over. "Mama, Papa," she said, but before she could finish, one of the young female assistant said, "Emma Sinead, you were on all the television stations and papers in Argentina." Emma Sinead blushed, but then quickly recovering her composure, she smiled and said, "Yes, it was a big surprise for me. I thank you so much for being here, I miss our national food."

Later, as Ellinor sat in the lounge with Nadia, they spoke about their childhood and their children. As Nadia spoke, she looked over to Nikita and said, "We are truly blessed in having such a beautiful and intelligent daughter. Ellinor, I feel sure you think the very same about Emma Sinead."

"Yes," she replied. "She is a light into our life, and as I watch her grow, it gives me a great feeling of happiness."

Nadia said thoughtfully, "When you see all the girls together, they look and behave like sisters and look at them now, laughing and chattering."

Soon they were joined by Jose, Anabella and Alex. "Ellinor, I had a call a short time ago, from Peter O'Houlihan," Alex said. "He was so happy to talk with you."

"That was very good of him," said Ellinor, "he sounded a really nice person. I suggested he contact you to discuss any plans there may be."

"Well," Alex replied, "I have suggested that we meet in my hotel, The Forge tomorrow evening."

The good doctor, feeling that he had to acknowledge the huge debt, said, "Alex, we do not want to impose too much on your hospitality, also, I need to reimburse you for all the expenses you have had in taking us to Scotland and bringing us here. After all, you are here on business, not to ferry us round." "Jose, it is not a problem," replied Alex, "I mix a little pleasure with my business and we enjoy your families' company." He continued, "Believe me, this trip is as important to my family as it is to your family. So, let's not discuss expenses any further. Now! that's settled, tomorrow we will take you to visit the city of Limerick and then on to Nenagh."

Alex asked Jose, "Would you and your family, and of course Emma Sinead, like to meet with a few of the locals and some of the local press this evening? A small group, an informal evening, no speeches, just some guests." Jose looked to his wife, "That would be very nice."

"Good!" said Alex. He called the waiter over, "Could you please tell Mr Ahern to go ahead with his plans for this evening?"

"I'll do it right now sir," the waiter answered. "And on your way back, could you bring the good doctor a pint of Guinness?"

"Of course sir," the waiter replied, and walked directly to Mr Ahern's office, returning shortly with the Guinness, he handed the glass to Jose.

"I have never drunk a black beer before," Jose said, and as he put the glass to his lips, the five girls appeared. "Papa!" Emma Sinead blurted out, "are you going to drink that?"

"We are trying to turn your father into an Irishman!" answered Alex. Looking at her father, Emma Sinead asked if she could smell the beer. She put her nose close to the glass, her father raised the glass a little, leaving some of the froth on her nose. "Papa, it smells terrible!" When she turned round, everyone laughed. "Look at your face, Emma Sinead!" Alessia exclaimed, pointing at her nose.

Emma Sinead rushed over to the large mirror hanging on the wall, and came running back quickly, her cheeks bright red, "Mama, Papa, it is so embarrassing! People will think I'm drinking beer!"

Her mother handed her a tissue and asked, "Are all you girls going to the pool later?"

"Yes Mama," was the reply from Emma Sinead, "but first, Mr Ahern is going to take us round the castle, to see the ghosts." As the girls were about to leave, Nadia said, "Ladies, we have to be down here in the reception at seventeen thirty. All looking your best."

"Ok, see you later!" was the general reply.

At Seventeen fifteen, everyone waited in the reception for Patrick Ahern to arrive. "Ladies, you are all looking beautiful!" he commented. "In a moment, we will go into the main lounge and meet our guests." Patrick opened the large double doors leading to the lounge area.

Emma Sinead was surprised as the lounge was almost full. Holding her mother's arm, she walked through the doors, immediately there was the flash of cameras and generous applause. Alex stepped forward and guided the Salvador family to the front. He said loudly, "Mr and Mrs de Salvador, and of course Emma Sinead de Salvador, may I introduce you to the Argentinean Ambassador to Ireland, Mrs Silvia Merega."

The Ambassador, holding Emma Sinead's hand tightly said, "You, Emma Sinead de Salvador, have made your country so proud of you." Then turning to Jose, Ellinor and Anabella, "I am sure you have never been more proud of Emma Sinead than right now."

Jose replied, "She is the light and inspiration of our life."

The Ambassador walked with the Salvador family and introduced them to the press and the other guests. As they walked round the room, Alex Andrusanke spoke in his booming voice, "I would like to ask the members of the press to be respectful of whom they are talking to, she is a young lady and not an adult!"

The meeting with the press lasted round thirty minutes. When they walked from the lounge, Patrick Ahern approached Alex and whispered, "Everything is ready, if you would like to take your group into the main conference hall where a special dinner had been organised." As they left the lounge, Alex thanked everyone for coming and guided his family and friends into the conference centre where they approached the extra large table in the middle of the room. Patrick Ahern called out, "My friends, can I ask you to please sit opposite your name tag." As they sat down, they noticed that there were two vacant seats next to each of the three girls. Alex stood up and spoke. "When Jose and Ellinor de Salvador and their beautiful daughter, Emma Sinead, decided to come to the United Kingdom for a medical conference, they never envisaged the changes that this trip would make to their lives and to our lives." Alex continued, "My wife Nadia, would now like to say a few words."

Nadia stood up and tapped her wine glass. "Attention please," she said. "I would like to start with the friends of my daughter Nikita. Andrea, Saya, and Alessia. My husband and I, and with the help of the Argentine ambassador, have organised a little private surprise for all three of you."

The room was in complete silence, when suddenly the doors at the end of the room opened. Saya was the first to speak, "Oh my God! It's my mother and father!" Then running to meet them, and greeting them in the Japanese tradition by bowing.

Andrea looked up, "Mama! Papa!" as she jumped up to greet them and finally, Alessia, with tears in her eyes ran to greet her parents. The conference hall was buzzing with chatter. Nadia introduced the unexpected guests to the Salvador family. Emma Sinead turned to her mother and grandmother and said, "Now the family is complete."

At around midnight, Alex called for everyone's attention. "Tomorrow, we have a fairly busy day. Early in the morning, we are being taken on a tour of the City of Limerick organised by my good friend, Mr Patrick Ahern." Immediately, everyone applauded, he continued, "And in the afternoon, we travel to Nenagh, which is about 24 miles north of Limerick. We will spend one or two nights at the Abbey Field Hotel in Nenagh, and later at around 15:00 hours, we travel five miles to my hotel and restaurant near Lough Derg. A small hotel called The Forge, where Emma Sinead, and her family will meet their Irish cousins."

On their way to their rooms, Anabella spoke with smiling eyes, "Emma Sinead and Andrea, no talking all night, you young girls need all your beauty sleep." The two girls laughed as they made their way to the lift.

Chapter 26

Early next morning Alex, Nadia and Patrick Ahern were already in the dining hall with the parents of Andrea, Saya, and Alessia, when the Salvador family arrived. "Good morning, Anabella, Ellinor, and of course, Jose! I hope you had a pleasant night's sleep?" Alex asked.

Jose replied smiling, "Eventually, after all the talking died down."

"Please sit here," Patrick said, as he pulled out the chair by his side.

Alex said laughingly, "I expect the five ladies will be using their feminine rights and be late!" The door opened and in came the five beautiful ladies. "*Hola!*" Andrea said to the room in general. "*Buongiorno*," said Alessia as she walked over to greet her parents. "Good morning, everyone," said the smiling Nikita, "I hope you all slept well."

"*Ohayo*," Saya said as she gave the traditional Japanese bow to everyone, and especially to her parents. Emma Sinead, the last one in, "*Buenos dias a todos*," she walked over to her family and gave each one of them a kiss on the cheek. As they sat down, Ellinor remarked to her husband, "They are all so pretty and look at our Emma Sinead!" she reached out and held her daughters hand. "The dress, it's beautiful on you," she said. Emma Sinead replied, "Thank you, Mama." She then threw her arms round her grandmother. "Grandmama," she said, "I am so happy today!"

"Why today?" asked her mother, wondering if Emma Sinead knew anything. She looked at her mother, "All our family are here," she said, and in a soft voice, "even great grandad."

Emma Sinead stood up, "Do you like my dress, Papa?"

"It's beautiful, you look just like a princess! *Estoy Sin plabras te parezco a un modelo*," her father replied, then he laughed. "But I am not sure which one of you five girls I would take to the dance."

"Of course you would choose me," Emma Sinead laughingly replied.

"I would be a proud father to escort you to the dance, my dear."

"We will all come with you," said Andrea. "Can you imagine?" laughed Ellinor, "what the people of Buenos Aries would think, if you escorted all those five beautiful girls to the local dance?"

Anabella turned to Emma Sinead, "Now, you look just like your great-grandmother, Isabela, when she was your age."

"Grandmamma," said Emma Sinead, "I have seen photographs of great-grandmother when she was young, she was so beautiful."

"She was beautiful, and loved your great-grandfather very much," replied Anabella.

Alex warned them, "Our transport to Nenagh will be outside in a few moments, so after breakfast, please make you way to reception."

Patrick Ahern was there to see them off. He reached out and took the hand of Jose, "It has been a great pleasure meeting you and your family, and I hope you return to our country and, of course, this hotel again." Jose thanked him for his hospitality. Patrick turned to Ellinor and her mother, "It was a pleasure having you as guests in my hotel and now you know where Ireland and Bunratty Castle are, I expect you to return again soon." Anabella replying, said, "I cannot thank you enough for your hospitality and the friendship you have shown to my family."

"It was my pleasure," replied Patrick as he kissed her hand. He then turned to face all the girls, "You five ladies, brought a light of happiness to this hotel." And turning directly to Emma Sinead, "The staff of Bunratty Hotel put their hands in their pockets, and bought you a little gift. Something for you to remember your visit to the Bunratty Castle Hotel." He handed Emma Sinead a gift-wrapped box. She opened it, and exclaimed, "Oh my God, it is beautiful!" as she took out a small golden Celtic cross.

"Please allow me," Patrick said, as he took the cross and pinned it to the lapel of her dress. Emma Sinead quickly turned to her family, "Mama, Papa, Grandmamma, look! It is very beautiful." She then walked over and thanked the girls behind the reception desk.

Patrick called Alex aside, "I will see you at the Abbey and I will be bringing a few guests."

"That's good," replied Alex. "I presume all the guests will be Celts."

"But of course," he answered, "all true Celts and ready to protect the tradition."

With the passengers on board the two coaches, they made their way on the M18. Heading in the direction of Limerick, two police cars came up from behind and took up position on the road in front of the coaches.

"Mama," said Emma Sinead, "I think we are going to meet the Queen of Ireland!" as she pointed to the two police cars.

"I think someone knows you are here, Emma Sinead," answered Nadia.

Soon they were heading down the M7 towards Nenagh. Emma Sinead's grandmother sat next to her on the coach and holding her hand, she produced a small package from her bag and placed it firmly in Emma Sinead's hand. "Tomorrow, you will place the contents of this little box under the soil at your great-grandfather's family grave. Inside, there is a sealed written letter from your great-grandfather. You must read the letter out loud for their spirits to hear the words. Your great-grandparents will be so proud of you."

Emma Sinead held the box tightly and not wanting to ask what the contents were, she replied, "Yes Grandmama, I will do that. Shall I also place the lock of hair that Mama gave me in the same place?"

"No, my dear," her grandmother answered, "you will find another fitting place for that."

"Grandmama, how will I know when I find the correct place?"

"In your heart you will know my child, just wait and see," answered her grandmother. "Will you tell me, Grandmama, if I choose the wrong place?" Emma Sinead asked. "Do not worry my child," her grandmother gently replied, "you will make the correct decision."

The two Mercedes coaches made their way along the M7, and soon they were turning off on to the old Limerick road to enter the town of Nenagh. Both coaches entered the grounds of the Abbey Field Hotel, only the top management of the hotel being aware of the guest list. Alex walked with the group to the hotel reception. The manageress, Mrs Mary Clifford, greeted them. Word of the arrival of Emma Sinead spread round the town quickly, and that evening, there was a sudden increased booking for dinner from locals, hoping to see and possibly meet with Emma Sinead.

The five girls decided to make full use of the hotel leisure facilities. Emma Sinead, Andrea and Alessia made their way to the swimming pool. Nikita and Saya went to the gym. Alex Andrusanke now had the opportunity to sit and discuss with the family, the plans for the evening ahead and the trip the following day to Holy Cross Abbey. The telephone rang, Alex answered. "Hello, Andrusanke here."

"Sorry to bother you, Mr Andrusanke, this is reception, will your party be having dinner in the hotel tonight?"

Alex replied, "We are attending a private reception in my hotel at Ballycommon, and will be late back."

"That's fine then," replied the receptionist. The doorbell rang, Nadia opened the door. "Alessia, is something wrong?"

"No, no" she said, "but I think someone needs to go down to reception. There are many schoolchildren wanting to talk with Emma Sinead and asking her for her autograph."

"Ok, we will come down," replied Nadia. When they reached the reception, it was full of children, all very quiet and paying full attention to Emma Sinead, who was explaining her meeting with the Queen, and telling them all about her country Argentina. Ellinor and Jose just stood and listened to their daughter, who had just turned thirteen. Jose looked to his wife and whispered, "Is that the same shy, young girl we brought over from Buenos Aires, just a few weeks ago? She is so full of confidence."

"I can now see clearly everything mother told us last evening." Ellinor answered, "She is indeed special!"

Alex and Mrs Clifford took control of the situation and took all the children into the main hall. Alex in his booming Russian voice, spoke, "Now, boys and girls, if you remain very quiet and with lots of good behaviour, I will ask all five beautiful girls to come and talk to you, just as soon as they have changed."

A loud cheer went up, the door opened, and the receptionist ushered in another small group. The manageress, Mrs Mary Clifford, spoke to the receptionist quietly, "Can you tell anyone else who arrives, that Emma Sinead and her friends are resting?"

Ellinor, Anabella and Nadia walked round, talking to the children and keeping them busy, while the girls changed and Alex ordered a table with cakes and soft drinks for the children.

After around 10 minutes, the door opened and in walked Emma Sinead and the four girls, followed by the parents of Andrea, Alessia and Saya. The room was buzzing with excitement, questions coming from every corner. Alex took charge, placing the children into groups, each of the five girls would spend a little time with each group.

Saya was busy talking with a small group, when a young girl looked at her and said, "I have seen you on television, Miss."

"On television?" Saya asked, "Yes," the girl replied, "you were climbing a big mountain and you had no ropes. Are you not afraid you will fall?"

"You are one very observant young lady!" replied Saya.

"My daddy saw it too!" the young girl replied. "He said you were crazy!" Saya laughed and gave the girl a big embrace and whispered in her ear, "Sometimes, I think I am crazy, but please do not tell anyone." The girl looked at Saya and asked, "Would you like to come to my school and visit my class?"

Saya smiled, "Thank you very much for the invitation," she answered, "I do not think we will have the time, but I will check." The young girl handed Saya a piece of paper, and said, "That is my name," pointing to her name on the paper. "Kathryn Quirke, the name, address of my school and my class." And holding Saya's hand she said, "I hope you can come."

"I will try my best Miss Kathryn," replied Saya.

The meeting with the children lasted around 45 minutes and all the boys and girls eventually left the hotel. Alex turned to Jose and said, "I have never seen so many excited children in my whole life," then turning to the five girls, he joked, "now you know what I go through every time I go out!" Everyone laughed.

Saya had told Nikita about the young girl's invitation, and she decided to ask her father if there would be time for a quick visit to the school. Alex Andrusanke spoke to Saya, regarding the possible visit to a school and he agreed that he would look at the schedule after the visit to the Abbey. Emma Sinead hesitantly spoke up, "Grandmama, can I ask you a question?"

"Oh dear, this sounds serious!" her grandmother replied.

"No, it's not serious," replied Emma Sinead, she continued, "yesterday, Nikita and the girls were talking. They were speaking in their own languages. Just like in my dream."

"That's pretty normal my dear," replied her grandmother. "Just think how many times since you have been here, have you spoken in Spanish to English people?"

"I know Grandmama," replied Emma Sinead, "but I can understand them, just as if they were speaking Spanish." Her mother interrupted,

"Sometimes, Emma Sinead, when you hear people talking in a different language, you can understand a person from the actions and the tone of their voice."

"Mama," replied Emma Sinead, "it's not that, I know what they are talking about, it's the same as if they were speaking Spanish and they also understand each other." Her grandmother held Emma Sinead by the hand. "You, my dear, are the great-grandchild of a very humble man who left this country in search of a new life. He was born into the Celtic race, people who were great believers in mythology and science. Information was so important for their daily life, they studied the movement of stars across the night sky, and soon realised that the same stars appeared regularly. They strongly believed a supreme force controlled the stars, and that it ruled their lives." She continued, "You, my dear, have inherited some of your great-grandfather's abilities and tradition." Then, squeezing Emma Sinead's hand, said softly, "You take after your great-grandfather, you are a true Celt. Your ability to learn and study situations will be one of your greatest assets in your life. Does that answer your question my dear?"

"Yes, Grandmama."

Emma Sinead's mother was about to say something, when the phone rang. It was Alex telling them that they would be leaving the hotel in forty-five minutes.

"Thank you, Alex," Ellinor replied, "we will be ready." Ellinor turned to Emma Sinead, "The next time I hear the girls talking together, I will pay more attention. But now, I think we should get ready, we leave here in a short time."

Chapter 27

At 15:00 hrs, Alex and his guests drove out of Nenagh for the short drive to the Forge Hotel at Ballycommon. The Manageress, Mrs Rose and her assistant were out in the parking lot to greet them on their arrival. Alex walked ahead, leaving the rest of the group in the hands of the Manageress.

He walked through the reception area and directly to the main dining hall, checking everything was in place for the gathering of the relatives. Calling to the headwaiter, he asked, "Could you please remove any tables that will not be used, it will give more space." He turned and walked quickly back to the reception. The receptionist greeted him, "Good evening Mr Andrusanke, we are so fortunate with the weather today, it is excellent." He replied, "Since we arrived in Ireland, God has blessed us with beautiful weather and let's hope it lasts, but Ireland has changeable moods when it comes to the weather." He continued, "Are the kitchen staff and waiters all prepared?"

"Yes sir," the receptionist replied, "everything has been done as you requested."

The Salvador family and friends made their way into the main reception. Alex stood there and greeted them, "I would like to welcome all of you to my little hotel, The Forge, and as it is now 15:45, I would suggest we meet here at 19:30 hrs. There are some lovely walks round the village, just feel free to do whatever pleases you." Alex and his wife then left and made their way to the kitchen.

The manageress, Mrs Rose, took the group into the main lounge which had two patio doors leading out to a very large glass covered conservatory, overlooking freshly ploughed fields.

Jose sat down and called to his wife, "Ellinor, I think we should all go for a good long walk before our Irish cousins arrive."

"That sounds like a good idea," Ellinor replied, and turned to her mother, "would you like to come with us, mother to explore the village?"

"Of course," Anabella replied, "It's a beautiful evening. It reminds me of a summer's evening in Buenos Aries. Let's ask the others to join us."

"Mama," Emma Sinead asked, "can I go with the girls and explore the village?"

"Of course," answered her mother. "But don't get lost!" The waiter, who was standing close by, laughed, "That's not possible in Ballycommon ma'm." Ellinor replied, laughing, "Our five girls could get lost in one room!"

The girls made their way out of the hotel and immediately had a difficult decision to make. Left, right, straight on or back? They decided to turn right and almost immediately met the local priest, who was just about to get into his car, and recognising Emma Sinead, he spoke to them. "If I am not mistaken, you are the young lady whose photograph is in every Irish paper." The five girls, surprised by his voice, turned. He spoke again, "My name is father Hamilton. It's a great pleasure to meet you, Emma Sinead de Salvador and your friends." Emma Sinead introduced the four girls to the priest. He talked with all five girls for a few minutes and then spoke directly to Emma Sinead. "I have a book in my church, and I am sure you would be interested in seeing the contents."

"Where is your church?" asked Nikita. "Just a short distance towards the lake, about one mile," he answered. "We could walk there," said Emma Sinead. "Better still," said the priest, "I can take you in my car and bring you back."

"Ok," was the reply as they climbed into his car. Soon after, they veered off the main road and drove up a slight hill. As they reached the top, on the left side, was the village school and alongside, the church. The priest spoke, as he drove through the freshly painted cast iron gates, "Welcome to St. Mary's Church of Carrig." Emma Sinead, remembering the name Carrig and what her grandmother had told her asked, "Is this great-grandfather O'Houlihan's church?"

"It is indeed!" replied the priest. "Your great-grandfather was christened right here," he said, pointing to the christening font by the side altar. "He had his first communion here and his confirmation." He continued, as they walked towards the altar, "Life was hard, especially on a tied farm with bad land. Leaving the country was sometimes the only choice."

"What is a tied farm?" asked Saya, "It is a farm that is rented to the user,

123

and usually the land is bad," the priest replied. "Please sit," he said, as he pointed to the row of pews.

"I will be back in a moment," he said, as he as he walked into the sacristy, rapidly returning with a large book. He placed the book on the wide altar rail and flipped through the pages.

"Please," he said, inviting them to come and look at the book. Emma Sinead looked and there, written in faded ink, was the name of her great-grandfather, Thomas James O'Houlihan: Christened on January 5th, 1898. "My God, it's my great-grandfather!" Emma Sinead said, as she touched the writing on the book. She looked up and asked, "Can you bring the book to the hotel, so my grandmother can see this?" The priest answered, "Normally, the book should stay in the church, but on this special occasion, I will bring the book this evening for your grandmother and mother to see." He continued, "There is something else I would like you to see." He took them to the christening font alongside the side altar. "Your great-grandfather was christened right here at this very font. His mother and father, your great great-grandmother and great great-grandfather, would have stood here on either side holding the newborn O'Houlihan."

Emma Sinead placed her hand on the font and glancing down, she noticed a tiny wooden panel on the side of the font. "What's this door for?" she asked, pointing to the side panel. The priest looked down, "You have a keen eye, Emma Sinead, I had never noticed that before." He tugged at the panel, which was no bigger than a letter box. It opened, and peering in, he said, "There is nothing inside."

"Father!" Emma Sinead said, as she reached into her bag and pulled out the little box her mother had given her many years ago. She opened the box and showed the contents and photograph to the priest.

"He was just a young boy then," the priest said.

Emma Sinead answered, "This picture was taken just three days after he arrived in Argentina." She opened the little package, it contained a lock of hair and a tooth. "Padre O'Daley cut his hair a few days after he arrived," she said. Father Hamilton joked, "Did he also pull the tooth?" she smiled, "I don't know father, maybe he did." Father Hamilton was almost speechless and simply said, "After all this time, Thomas O'Houlihan, you have truly come home." Emma Sinead spoke in a commanding voice, "This box belongs here!" As she placed the box into the little opening. "Father!" she said, "my grandmother was right, she told me when I find the place for the box, it will be the right place." As the priest closed the little door, he noticed a faint green glow coming from the inside. But when he looked again, it had vanished, he just smiled. All five girls stayed in the church for a few more minutes. After the priest returned the book to the sacristy, he then drove them the short distance back to the village, and promised Emma Sinead he would bring the book to the hotel that evening.

The Salvador family and the parents of Saya, Alessia and Andrea walked through the village. They came to a narrow tree-lined track, and decided to explore. They had only walked a short distance when the five girls arrived and joined them. They all continued walking slowly along the track. Emma Sinead reached out and held her grandmother's hand. "Grandmama," she whispered, "great-grandfather was here!" Before her grandmother could answer, they came to an opening, and were facing the front of an abandoned stone built building, with a large tree growing alongside its entrance. Most of the thatched roof had collapsed, and all that remained on top was a stone chimney, which was leaning precariously to one side. Emma Sinead walked towards the building. Ellinor called out in alarm, "Emma Sinead! Be careful, it may fall on you!" At that moment, a woman came walking down the track. "Can I help you?" she asked. Emma Sinead replied, "Was this ruined building a house?"

"It was, many years ago," the woman replied. "Built before the eighteen hundreds, an English family owned this cottage and the big house where I live. When I purchased the properties several years ago, on the deeds there had been many owners. I noticed on the land records, this cottage and some land at the back had been rented to a family, I think the name was O'Houlihan, but that was many, many years ago. I don't know what happened to them."

Suddenly, Anabella said she felt faint. "Mother, are you all right?" asked Ellinor, "You look pale." Jose, who was standing in front, came back quickly. "Anabella, please sit here," he said, pointing to the low wall. He proceeded to check her pulse. "Jose, I'm ok. Yes. I'm fine," she said.

"Are you sure?" Jose asked.

"I have never felt happier in my whole life!" she said. Jose looked at her, confused, "This is the birthplace of my father, Thomas O'Houlihan."

"How do you know?" asked Jose. "Emma Sinead knows," she replied, "she can feel his presence."

"Yes, Papa," Emma Sinead said, as she walked towards what was the only entrance to the building, and standing beside the large tree, she placed her hand on the wall of the cottage. "His spirit is here," she said, then turning to her grandmother, "Grandmama! Please come here quickly," she said as she held out her hand. Anabella walked over and placed her trembling hand in the outstretched hand of her granddaughter. "Place your hand on the wall, Grandmama," Anabella placed her outstretched hand on the wall of the old building.

"My God! I hear his voice!" She looked towards her daughter, Ellinor. "Ellinor! I can hear him! I can hear my father talking to me! Can you imagine?"

Just as she spoke, the large tree they were standing beside burst into life. Beautiful pink cherry blossoms expanded out of nowhere, and falling all around like pink snowflakes. Anabella, holding her hands in the air to catch the falling flowers, looked to her granddaughter and said, "It's just like your grandfather used to say. When springtime comes, the pink flowers will fall like snow and bless the world."

Saya, looking up at the falling blossoms, spoke, "It's just like the island of Hokkaido in Japan. It's beautiful!" The ground surrounding the tree was now covered in pink flowers. Anabella stooped down and picked one of the flowers, carefully placing it in her bag.

They thanked the woman for allowing them on her property. She was silent for a moment, and then said in an excited voice, "I have never seen anything like that in my whole life! I cannot remember ever seeing that tree in flower!" Emma Sinead walked over and held the woman's hand, she explained how important it had been for her grandmother to see the cottage, and thanked her again. Then they made their way back down the track. As they walked, Anabella held Emma Sinead's hand tightly and said to her, "Your great-grandfather told me you found the right place, you have fulfilled the promise."

Emma Sinead answered, "Yes, Grandmama, I found the right place." Her grandmother smiled and said, "I never doubted you, my child," as she placed her arm round her grandaughters shoulder.

"Grandmama! Mama!" Emma Sinead blurted out in an excited voice, "I forgot to tell you! We saw the christening book, and great-grandfather's name is in it!" She then proceeded to explain everything that had happened. "Grandmama! The priest will bring the great book to the hotel this evening." Jose spoke up, "I think we should all make our way back to the hotel now, I think Anabella needs a rest."

After they entered the hotel, Jose asked Alex if there was a room which Anabella could rest in for a short time. Alex organised a room immediately.

Emma Sinead went with her grandmother to the room, and talked about their discoveries. She explained to her grandmother the whole story from start to finish, the little church in Carrig, and the meeting with the priest. Anabella took her grandaughter's hand, "I could never have imagined in my whole life what happened today, just think! We stood at your great-grandfather's house."

"Grandmama! You are trembling! I will call Papa."

"No, it is ok my child," she replied, "when you held my hand at the old house, I heard his voice."

"Grandmama, please let me get Papa," Emma Sinead said as she rushed out the door. Jose and Ellinor came in quickly. Ellinor held her mother's hand.

"Ellinor," Anabella said, "he talked to me and told me he is watching over us." Jose examined Anabella quickly. "I think you are ok, he said. Maybe a little shock when you saw your father's house."

"Jose, he told me to explain the necklace to you and especially to Emma Sinead, please sit down."

Emma Sinead and Ellinor sat on each side of Anabella. Jose sat by the window. Anabella asked Emma Sinead to remove her necklace, and to place it carefully on the table. She pointed to the diamond in the centre, "This is your Birthstone, these are also Birthstones." Pointing to the other four stones, "They are positioned like the numbers on a clock." She continued, looking to her granddaughter, "Emma Sinead, you know, there are five necklaces in all, and each necklace has a different birthstone in the centre." Anabella continued in a soft voice, and told Emma Sinead about the magic of the necklace. "The necklace will turn invisible when you are in danger, but it will still be round your neck. When you need help, just touch your birthstone and think of the girls. They will come to you and if you just need one girl, just touch her Birthstone." She continued, "Let me place the necklace round your neck," and after a moment, "now, Emma Sinead, touch the Birthstone on the right of the centre stone." Raising her hand slowly, she touched the birth stone on the right. The room was immediately bathed in a green glow. "Grandmama," she said, "I heard Andrea's voice, and she is coming here now."

A few seconds later, Andrea appeared out of nowhere in the room.

"Are you all right, Emma Sinead?" she asked.

"I am fine," Emma Sinead answered, "I am sorry Andrea, it was Grandmama, she is teaching me all about the magic necklace." Andrea said nothing, just smiled.

Jose and Ellinor just sat there totally surprised by what had just happened.

"I am fine now," Anabella remarked. As she held her granddaughters hand, she continued, "The four girls will always be there for you." Anabella waited for Emma Sinead to respond. Emma Sinead finally spoke, "Grandmama! You mean, the girls and Andrea are like my sisters?"

"Yes, just like sisters," replied her grandmother. Emma Sinead turned to Andrea, "You knew all of this?"

"Yes," Andrea replied, "but we could not tell you, it was important you had to find these things out by yourself." There was a sudden flash, and Andrea was gone. All Emma Sinead could say was, "Wow!"

Giving her grandmother a kiss on the cheek, Emma Sinead said, "I knew this was going to be the best day of my life, thank you, Grandmama."

"There is much more to learn," her grandmother said in a soft voice, "your new found sisters will guide you, but now let's go and meet our guests."

They walked out of the room, along a short corridor and into the lounge. The first introduction was to Mr Peter O'Houlihan and his family. As she looked around the lounge, Anabella said in amazement, "I never realised we had so many distant cousins here."

"Well, from what I see, it is more like hundreds," replied Jose.

"Ellinor," Anabella said, "you look a little upset."

Ellinor answered with a question that had been bothering her for a little while, "Mother, why did you not tell us about the necklace before and what Andrea just did, she just appeared and disappeared, how is this possible? Is it normal?"

Anabella put her arm round Ellinor's shoulder, "There is a right time for everything. When we were at fathers house, he told me, now is the time to tell all." "Ellinor, later this evening when we return to our hotel I will tell you all that I know." Then, pointing to Emma Sinead, who was with her new-found sisters and Peter O'Houlihan's daughter, remarked, "Look at her, Ellinor! She is so happy to have four new friends, I should say four new sisters! It is her destiny and they will protect each other."

As they were speaking, the local parish priest walked into the lounge with a large book under his arm. He smiled as he approached Ellinor and Anabella, "I can tell by looking, you are mother and daughter." Both Anabella and Ellinor looked up. "I am Father Hamilton from the local church in the parish of Carrig." Both women attempted to stand, "Please remain seated, ladies," Father Hamilton said, indicating with his hand.

By this time, Alex had walked over and introduced himself.

"I am very pleased to meet with you, Mr Andrusanke, and delighted to see the Forge Hotel open for business again." He paused, "Mr Andrusanke, I have a very large book here to show Doctor de Salvador and these wonderful ladies, and also to have a little chat with them about a great man, Thomas O'Houlihan."

"Please," responded Alex, "use my office it will be much quieter." Anabella, Ellinor and Jose followed Alex and the priest. "Just make yourselves at home here," said Alex as he closed the door, then walked back to the lounge area.

Father Hamilton first chatted about Emma Sinead and her four friends, then, placing the book on the large polished table, he carefully opened the first page. There it was, the written record of Thomas O'Houlihan's christening. Anabella sat for a moment in silence, a smile on her face. "I never imagined, one day I would see my father's christening record, together with the names and the marks of his parents."

"I understand from the marks the parents made, neither could read or write," said the priest.

"Seeing this brings him much closer to me," replied Anabella as she looked at the priest, "Father, he never met his granddaughter Ellinor, or his great-granddaughter Emma Sinead, that is, until this day."

Father Hamilton interrupted, "I am sure after today, Thomas James O'Houlihan knows you are here." He continued to turn the pages, "he knows we are here," replied Anabella, softly. Ellinor held her mother's hand as Father Hamilton spoke, "these are the records of your father, Thomas James O'Houlihan, having his first communion and his confirmation." He continued to turn the pages, "And finally, the death records of both his parents, with a note saying they were both interred at Holy Cross Abbey in the County of Tipperary." Jose, his wife Ellinor, and Anabella sat in stunned silence. Father Hamilton spoke as he opened a large brown envelope, "This came from the school archives." He placed an old faded photograph, yellow and cracked, on the table.

Anabella spoke first, "Oh my God! Look at the photograph. He's so cute! Is he really my father?" she asked, pointing to the photograph. "He's no more than six years old."

"He was seven years old," the priest answered. "This was the day of his first communion." He continued, "I am afraid, in those days, you came in the clothes you had. Now they buy designer clothes just for the occasion." Ellinor pointed at the photograph. "Look at his boots! They are all worn and dirty and he has no buttons on his jacket."

"But he is still cute!" remarked Anabella. "You know Ellinor, riches do not make the person." Father Hamilton said to them, "I will give copies of the pages and photograph, to take back to your home in Argentina."

"Thank you very much," Jose answered. "We never thought for one minute, when coming to England for a medical conference, that our lives would be altered like this. And to meet so many relatives we never knew we had." Father Hamilton replied, "It's a small world doctor, and if I may add, we are blessed to have your daughter Emma Sinead and her sisters visit us." As they walked out of the office towards the lounge, Anabella remarked, "It's gone so quiet." Just as she spoke, the haunting sound of pan pipes filled the room. Ellinor opened the door quietly, she could see Emma Sinead playing her pan pipes. The same tune she had been practising in their house in Buenos Aries.

"That is a beautiful piece of music," remarked Father Hamilton, "from a troubled time in Irish history."

"When we were children, my father, Thomas, used to whistle it all the time," said Anabella, "Mama Isabel always said, leave him alone now, he is thinking."

Just as Emma Sinead finished the first verse, Peter O'Houlihan's daughter stood up and began to sing the words, her voice resonating throughout the hotel. As she came to the last verse, the patrons in the two bars erupted into song. Peter O Houlihan's daughter stopped, but the singers in both bars continued, and when they eventually finished, there were loud cheers from the bars, and a voice shouted out loudly, "Three cheers for Thomas O'Houlihan. Hip! Hip! Horray! Hip! Hip! Horray!"

Jose looked surprised and turned to Father Hamilton, "How do they know of Thomas, was he famous?"

"It is a small world Dr. de Salvador," the priest replied. "Thomas O'Houlihan came from a very poor family, but his spirit and dreams are with your daughter." "It is indeed, a small world," replied Father Hamilton.

Peter O'Houlihan, sitting beside Emma Sinead and Ellinor, spoke, "It was a great honour to meet with all of you, our long-lost cousins from Argentina. I wish you all good health and happiness. I will meet with you tomorrow at the Abbey, so until then, I bid you all a safe journey back to Nenagh." Then, turning to Alex Andrusanke, "Alex, my friend, I have a busy day tomorrow and will now say goodnight. Alex, you have done a wonderful job bringing all these Celts together, and I know our work is just beginning."

Both bars, now full of locals, burst into song again with a second helping of Boolvogue, but this time, they marched into the lounge and stood round thetable where everyone was sitting. It was then, that Jose received his second pint of Guinness and looking at the glass, he saw the words *slainte* written in the froth of the beer. He looked over to Peter and asked, "What does this mean? How do they do it?" Peter answered amidst all the noise, "Jose, it means many things in Ireland, good health, safe journey, happiness and peace. The writing on the top takes many years of practise." Before Jose could answer, the Irish music started. Peter O'Houlihan stood up as if he was about to leave, he removed his coat and said, "I see we are not going home just yet." Three young lads appeared from the other bar, with a violin, banjo and accordion.

When the music began, all five girls danced and clapped to the delight of everyone in the room. Ellinor held Jose's hand, "My God," she said, "look everyone is smiling and happy."

Anabella answered, "Ellinor where ever they go peace and happiness will follow."

Emma Sinead had her first lesson in Irish dancing, from the daughter of Peter O'Houlihan. As she returned to the table out of breath, she asked, "Mama, did I do well?"

"You were just great," replied her mother. "Look at all the people smiling and happy, you and the four girls just light up the room."

Emma Sinead just looked at her mother and smiled at her choice of words.

Peter O'Houlihan spoke to her, "a few more lessons like that, Emma Sinead, and you'll be hopping round like a leprechaun."

"Have you seen a leprechaun? Mr O'Houlihan, I have read about them, I believe they are very mischievous little people."

"My dear," he replied, "you will be very fortunate if you ever meet one, and if you do, you must hold on to him tight and stop his escape. He will then be forced to give you three wishes. Now, to answer your question, Miss Emma Sinead, unfortunately I never got the opportunity to meet with a leprechaun."

Now, well after midnight, Alex stood up and called out in a loud voice, "Ladies and gentlemen! These five beautiful ladies have a very busy day tomorrow, and more important, I need my beauty sleep! So, we are going to bid you all good night, and safe journeys to your homes, but please do continue." They clambered into the coach and headed back to The Abbey Field Hotel.

After returning to the hotel, Emma Sinead had arranged to stay with Saya, which was a golden opportunity for Anabella to talk with Ellinor and Jose. Ellinor had made coffee and they sat round the table waiting for Anabella to begin.

"I will start at the beginning," Anabella said, "but first, I want you to step out onto the balcony." The three of them stood outside, Ellinor wondering what was coming next.

Anabella pointed up to the clear star filled sky. Ellinor looked up and said quietly, "I have never taken the time to stand outside our home at night and gaze in wonderment at the millions of stars."

Anabella gently spoke, "You have seen the stars carved on the stone slabs in Whitethorn Abbey." Then, pointing to a particular group of stars, "There! they are the stars known as The Pleiades or Seven Sisters."

"Yes, I see them!" said Ellinor, "Jose, can you see them?" she asked.

"Yes, I see them, the shape is identical to the carvings."

"Mother," Ellinor asked, "what have they to do with Emma Sinead or the other girls?" Anabella answered, "Let's go inside, It's getting a little chilly out here!"

They walked in and sat down, waiting for Anabella to continue.

"That's where they came from," she said. "Who, mother?" asked

Ellinor, "and from where? The stars?"

"The Angels," replied Anabella. She continued, "When your father died, and for many years after his passing, I wanted to go to him. I missed him so much, one night I placed all my pills on the table. I knew if I took them, it would be over and my heartbreak would stop. Suddenly, the room was filled with a green glow and before me, stood two beautiful girls, one much taller than the other. They were dressed in long white robes which had strange designs down the sides, now I know they were Celtic designs, then the taller of the two spoke. She said, "My name is Zani, I am an Angel of the Lord, and this is my daughter Gabriela.""

"For a moment, I thought I was dreaming," Anabella said, "until the Angel Zani spoke again. 'Anabella! It is not your time, soon you will be presented with a granddaughter, and with help from my daughter Gabriela, you will guide and protect her until her thirteenth year.' Both Angels bowed to me, and as suddenly as they appeared, they were gone. I looked at the pills on the table, scooped them up and threw them as hard as I could into the fire. One week later you telephoned me, and told me you were pregnant and it was a girl. Ellinor, you have no idea how I felt after you called me that day, and for weeks after your call. Every night, I would stand outside, look up at the night sky and say thank you."

"Mother, is all that you have told us true? Jose and I always thought you were a very strong person, and never realised you were so sad after father's death."

"Now I am very strong Ellinor. I still miss your father, but I know he is in a safe place and we will meet again. Now to continue, Ellinor, when Emma Sinead was born, you met Padre Alonso, by the way, the villagers in his parish were correct when they said he went with the Angels. He came to the hospital that day to prepare the way for Emma Sinead's journey. When you and Jose stood staring at her lifeless body, you thought all was lost, but for that brief moment, Emma Sinead was already with the Angels, who were preparing her for her future, and as quickly as they took her away, they brought her back to you. So, after thirteen years, and later today, just as they predicted at Holy Cross Abbey, she will be crowned the fifth Celtic Princess. Now it's late, and we must get some sleep," Anabella said.

"Mother! There are many questions I have to ask you!" said Ellinor.

"Ellinor! Jose! You already know the name of the group of stars, The Pleiades, but why did the Celts refer to them as the Seven Sisters?"

133

All Anabella said was, "Zani, Gabrelia, Nikita, Alessia, Andrea, Saya …… and Emma Sinead."

Chapter 28

The five girls were up early and made their way to the swimming pool. Andrea decided she would be first in the water and as the five approached, Andrea made a run and a quick dive into the pool. A large splash followed by a scream. She shouted out hoarsely, "The water is freezing, oh my God, it's so cold!"

Saya went to the edge and as she dipped her toe in the water, Alessia and Emma Sinead gave her a push, then swimming out to the centre, she remarked "Andrea, this is just like the water in Japan, very invigorating."

"You mean freezing!" stuttered Andrea. All five girls, now in the pool, decided to race. "Three lengths of the pool," said Nikita. So all five went to one end. "Are we ready? One, two, three," shouted Andrea, "and mind the icebergs!" It made no difference how fast either one of them swam, they were neck and neck all the way to the finish.

"Now Andrea, that was very invigorating!" laughed Saya. As the girls made their way back towards the reception area, the receptionist who had just come on duty, apologised. She had forgotten to inform them that the pool heating system was down for maintenance.

"That's ok," remarked Andrea, "we just pushed the icebergs out of our way."

"Ignore Andrea," laughed Alessia, "she was spoilt when she was a baby." The receptionist smiled apologetically.

Just then, Alex came in and looking at the five girls, he remarked, "You five have been up early." Nikita answered, "Father, we like to exercise before breakfast."

"Well, talking about breakfast," he answered as he turned to the receptionist,

"could you arrange a table for fourteen?"

"What time would you like to sit?" asked the receptionist.

Looking at his watch, he answered, "It's seven fifteen, I think eight o'clock would be fine."

"I will organise the tables for you right away," replied the receptionist.

All the families met in the dining hall at eight o'clock, the only ones missing were the Salvador family. Alessia turned to Nikita, "Something has happened," she said in a low voice, "I can feel sadness." Just then, the Salvador family came into the dining hall. Everyone could see Emma Sinead had been crying. As they approached, Ellinor spoke. "Just this morning, Emma Sinead received very bad news. Her best friend has been in a serious car accident and her family are not sure if she will survive."

The room was silent. Nikita came over to Emma Sinead gave her a hug and at the same time whispered in her ear, "Everything will be ok, we can fix it, wait and see." Emma Sinead looked at the other three girls, they smiled.

During breakfast, Emma Sinead whispered to her mother, "Mama, Maria will be ok now."

"I hope so," replied her mother. After breakfast, Jose approached Alex, "The information regarding Emma Sinead's friend is not good," he said. "We have not told Emma Sinead all the news. The doctors will switch off the life support machine just as soon as the girl's father arrives from Rio de Janeiro." Alex answered, "It is best not to tell her all the news. When we get to the Holy Cross Abbey we can all pray for her friend."

"Yes, I think you are right, it would only upset her more," answered Jose.

Breakfast over, they left the Abbey Field Hotel at 10:00 hrs, en route to Holy Cross Abbey, a journey of about one hour.

On arrival, the two coaches parked under the trees on the widened road overlooking the Abbey. Everyone made their way towards the Abbey entrance and Peter O'Houlihan approached from the entrance of the Abbey and spoke to them. "Good morning everyone, I do hope you had a pleasant drive from Nenagh. The honour has been given to me to guide you round this beautiful Abbey. And now if you would, please follow me."

Petre O'Houlihan spoke in his soft Irish accent. He asked for their attention and explained he would give them a brief history of the Abbey before entering.

"The Celtic name for the Abbey is *Uachtar-lamhan*. In 1168, Donal Mor O'Brien founded the monastery of the Benedictine order, building the Abbey on the site of an ancient Celtic place of worship. Years later, he transferred it to the Cistercians, then eventually it was colonised by monks from Monasteranenagh in the County of Limerick. In the year 1647, Oliver Cromwell arrived in Dublin, with instructions from Queen Elizabeth I to put an end to the catholics once and for all and in 1649 he ordered 20,000 troops to reduce every town to ashes. This included churches and monasteries. All because of Ireland's loyalty to the Pope, Holy Cross Abbey was destroyed and left in ruin. In 1969 an Act in the Irish Parliament made way for a full restoration project to begin. Sections of the Abbey were to be left unrestored, to enable visitors to see the mammoth task undertaken by the restorers."

They followed Peter as he walked slowly through the main entrance. Ellinor noticed the four girls, all of whom had dressed in green, with a small Celtic design embossed in gold on the front lapel. She remarked to Anabella how beautiful they looked.

Jose and Ellinor walked alongside Emma Sinead, who was wearing the two-tone green dress her grandmother had specially made for her, with a golden Celtic cross pinned on the lapel. Alex, carrying the carved stone tablet, walked behind his daughter Nikita. As they approached the arched door and entered the whitewashed stone entrance, Ellinor could already feel the peace and tranquillity emanating from the walls. They slowly made their way down the centre aisle of the main hall, the floor slightly inclined and paved with black and red quarry tiles giving the place a majestic feel.

The Abbey, divided into three sections by eight large sandstone pillars which stood like soldiers on either side of the main area, each two pillars supporting large hand-carved, arched wooden beams. Seventeen wooden pews on each side of the main aisle, with seventeen more on each side of the sandstone pillars. Peter, speaking in a whisper, explained, "In olden times, single ladies sat on the right and un-married men on the left. The centre area facing the main altar was usually reserved for married people and young children."

No one spoke as they walked down the aisle, their eyes drawn high up to the carved beams supporting the roof, which gave the Abbey a heavenly look.

Peter O'Houlihan remained silent. He wanted all of them to feel the magic of the Abbey, and the presence of God.

Patrick Ahern, already seated with a large group of people, each wearing a small Celtic symbol on their lapel. Patrick stood, walked over and joined Alex and Nadia as they walked down the aisle.

Anabella whispered to Ellinor, "It's so beautiful and peaceful, you can almost feel it!"

Emma Sinead turned to Alex, "I must carry the tablet now."

Alex carefully handed her the tablet, making sure she could manage the weight, then stepped aside.

Jose turned to his wife and spoke in a whisper, "This place is so magical. Look! there is someone kneeling at the altar." Ellinor looked to the side and could see a lone figure dressed in monk's robes, kneeling and facing the altar, with his hands joined in prayer. Alex and Patrick turned to the group and, pointing to the carved wooden seats in front, told them, "You must all sit here."

Jose, Ellinor, Nadia, Anabella along with the parents of Alessia, Andrea, and Saya sat in the front row of seats.

Emma Sinead walked slowly in front carrying the stone tablet, followed by the four girls. As they approached the altar, the four girls, without speaking or nodding, knelt on either side of the monk. Emma Sinead continued and walked through the open gates leading to the altar. She placed the stone tablet under the Celtic cross and knelt in prayer. Immediately, the Abbey bell chimed thirteen times, one chime for every year of her life.

Ellinor gripped her husband's hand tightly, and spoke softly, "I am so overcome with emotion and so happy."

On the thirteenth chime, the four girls stood, bowed to the Celtic cross, and walked through the altar gates to the sacristy beside the side altar.

Jose looked at his wife and said in a quiet voice, "It's like watching a movie or a play, they all know what they have to do."

Ellinor asked, "Where did our daughter learn this?"

"Her great-grandfather is guiding her," replied Anabella.

Emma Sinead stood up and slowly removed the necklace from around her neck, placing it carefully on the stone tablet. As she did so, the four girls walked out from the sacristy. Nikita in front, carrying what looked like another stone tablet, each of the four girls now wearing a golden tiara, which glistened in the sunlight coming through the stained-glass windows.

They approached the altar and walked towards Emma Sinead. Three of the girls stood by her side, Nikita stood behind for a moment, then walking forward carrying the second tablet, she stood in front of the Celtic cross. Carefully placing the stone tablet she was carrying alongside the one already there, the Abbey bell chimed out, as if in celebration.

Jose turned to Peter O'Houlihan and asked, "Peter, who is ringing the bell?"

"I don't know," was his reply. "That bell has been silent for hundreds of years and they never connected it to the ropes when they did the renovation." Speaking in a whisper, he continued, "They say when the Abbey bell chimes, it is to celebrate the inauguration of a princess."

On hearing the bell, people from round the village started to arrive at the Abbey and fill the seats behind. Alex stood and silently guided them to the rows of seats in the middle, making sure no one went past where his family were sitting.

Nikita walked from the altar towards Emma Sinead, holding out both her hands, which held the necklace. Ellinor turned to her husband, "Oh my God, it's just like the carving on the on the tablet!" Jose was silent and so intent on what was happening, he had not heard his wife talking to him.

Alessia stepped forward and placed a golden tiara on the head of Emma Sinead, and reaching out, she took the necklace from the hands of Nikita and placed it carefully round Emma Sinead's neck. Immediately a green glow, like an aurora borealis, surrounded the two tablets, expanding like a cloud until it filled every corner of the Abbey. The five girls now stood silently facing the congregation.

The lone figure kneeling at the altar stood up and walked towards the girls and bowed as he approached. Then, turning to face the congregation, he removed his hood.

Ellinor, taken by surprise, grabbed her husband's arm, "My God! It's Padre Alonso! He looks just like I saw him many years ago." Her husband whispered, "He is also the old man from the jewellery shop." An unearthly silence now penetrated the Abbey, and from high up in the beams, two green lights slowly descended and stopped in front of the five girls, transforming into two beautiful girls.

Anabella reached over and held Ellinor's hand tightly. "It's the Angels, Zani and Gabriela," she said in a low voice. Both Angels turned to face the five girls and bowed, then turning to face the congregation, the angel Zani spoke. "On this day, over two thousand years ago, a story was told and passed down from generation to generation of Celts. Now the prophecy has come to pass, and you bear witness to the crowning of the Fifth Celtic Princess."

Zani and Gabriela walked slowly towards the seated families and bowed. Gabriela reached out and held Anabella's hand, then placing a ring on Anabella's finger, she spoke, "This ring you know?"

Anabella, now gripping the ring with her other hand and twisting it round her finger, answered with a trembling voice, "Yes, I know it well," her eyes now filled with tears. The Angle Gabriela placed both her hands round Anabella's hands, gripping them tightly and spoke in a genteel voice, "He is safe with us." The green glow now covering the whole abbey got brighter. And, with a sudden flash, the two angels Zani and Gabriela were gone.

Padre Alonso asked the families to come forward.

As they walked towards the altar, Ellinor asked, "What ring is that, mother?"

Anabella held Ellinor's hand as she answered, "As they closed my husband's coffin," she paused for a long moment, then holding the ring with her other hand, she said, "I placed this ring on his finger. Now I know he is with them."

Ellinor put her arm round her mother's waist and said, "Thank you for being my mother."

Jose, his wife, Ellinor de Salvador and Anabella walked straight to Emma Sinead. Her mother hugged her tightly, almost crying and said, "I always knew you were special to me, but I never realised you were so special to the world."

Padre Alonso looked over to Ellinor, smiled and softly spoke to her, "Señora Ellinor de Salvador, after all of your years, we meet again."

"Padre Alonso," she replied, "both my husband and I, thank you and God for saving Emma Sinead's life. But there is much that we don't understand."

The Padre answered, "Señora de Salvador, there was no life to save, your daughter never died, she just went with the Angels for a brief moment of time and I hope after the events of today, you will understand a little more, but I assure you, Emma Sinead is in very safe hands and I know in time, you will see a clearer future for the world."

Ellinor introduced her husband, "This is my husband, doctor Jose de Salvador."

Padre Alonso smiled, reaching out and holding the doctor's hand, he spoke,

"A little shop in London was a strange place to meet doctor, I hope you are not too disappointed with the outcome?"

Jose replied, "Padre, what we have witnessed over the past few weeks and today, tells me that forces beyond our comprehension are looking after us, and I know my daughter Emma Sinead is in good hands."

Padre Alonso then spoke to Emma Sinead's grandmother, "Anabella Fernandez. All through the years that have gone by, you never lost faith or hope. Now your father's and mother's wishes are about to come true."

He then turned to Michael Hagen who was standing in the background, "Mr Hagen, sometimes governments and politics complicate simple issues and make the world ungovernable. Have faith in what you see."

Alex and Patrick Ahern walked towards the altar. The stone tablet was gone. Alex turned to Peter O'Houlihan "Peter! The tablet has gone."

On hearing this, Padre Alonso smiled and confided, "It has returned intact to its rightful place."

Padre Alonso walked with everyone out through a side door into a long, narrow covered passageway, the floor lined with the fallen tombstones of families long gone, their names sculptured into the stone. Carved wooden benches lined the rear wall, facing a large grassy courtyard, a place where monks would have sat, deep in meditation. Led by Padre Alonso, they walked in silence and eventually reached the section of the Abbey which had not been restored, entering through a small arched gateway. Emma Sinead now walked ahead, the four Princesses by her side and guided by the spirit of her great-grandfather, she stopped at an old headstone. The inscription read, 'Here lie the mortal remains of Jack and Annie O'Houlihan to await their salvation. RIP.'

The families had stopped a few meters back, the four Princesses stood behind Emma Sinead. She took the small box from her bag, opened it and removed a small brown envelope which was sealed with a blob of red wax. She knelt beside the grave and slowly pushed the remaining contents of the box into the soil. After a few moments she stood up, and facing the headstone, she carefully broke the seal on the envelope, removed the handwritten letter, and began to read out loud with a strong clear voice, a letter which had been written by her great-grandfather many years before. "To you Emma Sinead and all who stand here today at the graveside of my departed parents, your task almost complete. Our family united, you Emma Sinead, are now the fifth Celtic Princess, both Isabel and I, will always be with you." She then read out the name on the bottom of the letter, "Thomas James O'Houlihan."

When she had finished reading, her parents and grandmother came to her side and stood round the grave.

Anabella stood beside Emma Sinead and put her arm round her shoulder and said, "I do not know how your great-grandfather knew this day would come. He and my mother, Isabel, are now united with his parents."

Emma Sinead replied, "Grandmama, the task is not yet complete."

She reached down and scooped a little of the earth from the grave into the small box. "Grandmama," she said, "you must place this on their grave in Argentina. The task will then be complete."

"We will do that together one day," her grandmother answered.

As they walked back into the Abbey, led by Padre Alonso, and approached the main altar, Emma Sinead turned to her mother and said, "Mama, I have one more duty to perform. I must do this with the four Princesses."

Ellinor had never heard of the four girls being called Princesses and was surprised by her daughter's wording.

Emma Sinead and the four Princesses proceeded through the gate to the altar and walked towards the large Celtic cross. Emma Sinead in the centre, two Princesses on either side, they held hands and for a brief moment, a green glow filled the Abbey. The five Princesses stood up, turned and walked towards Padre Alonso. Nikita said, "Padre Alonso, our task is complete."

As they left the Abbey, Emma Sinead looked at her grandmother and said, "Now, my friend Maria will be fine."

Padre Alonso walked slowly over to the Salvador family. Emma Sinead held out her hand and gave a curtsy.

"Young Lady," Padre Alonso said as he bowed, "I should kneel before you! The Fifth Princess. I know the Gods have chosen wisely, you and the four Princesses will accomplish great things."

"Thank you, Padre Alonso," Emma Sinead responded.

Padre Alonso asked Jose, Ellinor and Anabella to join him, as he walked a short distance away from the rest of the group, and spoke with them at length.

By this time, the four Princesses had rejoined Emma Sinead.

Padre Alonso then excused himself and walked towards the five Princesses. He beckoned for them to walk with him as he made his way back towards the Abbey and sat down in the Cloisters overlooking the walled garden. The five Princesses sat with him, they talked for at least thirty minutes.

Outside, waiting by the coach, Peter O'Houlihan asked, "Where are the girls?"

"I believe they are with Padre Alonso," answered Jose. No sooner had the Doctor spoken, the five girls returned to the coach.

As Ellinor boarded the coach, she looked round, and asked, "Where Is Padre Alonso?"

Everyone looked round. Padre Alonso was nowhere to be seen.

"He will return if we need him, declared Saya."

Chapter 29

Mrs Martinez sat beside her daughter Maria's bed, holding and stroking her hand. The young girl's lifeless body lying, unresponsive to her mother's touch. Only a slight movement of her chest as the life support machine pumped oxygen into her lungs.

Every few minutes, a doctor or nurse would arrive and check the equipment was functioning correctly.

Mrs Martinez had been sitting there for almost one hour, when the doctor approached and asked her to come with him to his office. He sat behind a large desk, Mrs Martinez sat in front, staring at the wall behind the doctor. He spoke very softly so as not to upset her more than necessary.

"Mrs Martinez, I am sorry for what I have to tell you."

She looked at him with a questioning look in her eyes, "Maria is going to be fine?"

"No Mrs Martinez, your daughter's life has ended. It's the machine that is helping her to breath by putting air into her lungs." He continued, "She has suffered a massive injury to her head and now, after the results of the brain scan, I am afraid there is nothing more we can do."

Mrs Martinez sat in stunned silence, and after a few moments, she spoke. Pleading with the doctor, she blurted out, "Please! She is alive! She will come back to me."

The doctor reached out across the desk and held her hand, "Mrs Martinez, we all wish there was something more we could have done," then, realising she was getting more upset, he changed the subject to calm her down.

"Have you managed to contact your husband?" he asked. "Yes," she replied, "he is flying in from Rio this evening, I think at six o'clock."

The doctor told her, "I will arrange for someone to meet him, and bring him to the hospital."

"Thank you, doctor," Mrs Martinez replied. "Can I go now and sit with Maria?" He could see no point in prolonging the conversation, and decided it would be best to wait until her husband arrived.

"Yes, I think that will be all right," he replied.

The doctor left instructions for staff, there was to be no mention of switching the machine off until he returned. He would collect the father from the airport, this would give him the opportunity to prepare him for the worst.

Mr Martinez walked through the airport lounge at Buenos Aries International Airport, heading for the exit and taxi rank, when he saw a man standing, holding a card with his name on it.

"Excuse me, are you waiting for me?" he inquired. "Mr Martinez, on the flight from Rio de Janeiro?" the doctor asked. Mr Martinez confirmed that was he. The doctor introduced himself as he walked to his car. "Mr Martinez, we are going direct to the hospital."

As they drove towards the centre of the city, Mr Martinez, looking straight ahead at the lights of oncoming traffic, asked, "Is my daughter well? All that I know, is she was struck by a speeding car."

The doctor spoke with a sympathetic voice, "Mr Martinez, I am one of the doctors treating your daughter, and I am truly sorry, but I have bad news."

Without turning his head, he asked in a subdued voice, "Is my daughter dead?"

The doctor replied, "At the moment, she is connected to a life support machine, but after all our tests were completed, we cannot find any brain activity."

Mr Martinez sat, staring out at the moving traffic, wondering if this was all a dream, his eyes filling with tears. "Maybe she will wake, doctor," he said helplessly, "I have seen reports where that has happened."

"Yes, that has happened," the doctor replied, "In those cases there was life, the brain was working, but in Maria's case, there is no brain activity."

Mr Martinez continued to look straight ahead and, without turning to face the doctor, "what will happen now?" he enquired.

"We will give you some time to sit with your wife and Maria. I will return and ask you to leave the room. We will then remove all the tubes and make her look pretty. I will then call you when we have finished." The doctor continued with a sympathetic voice, "Mr Martinez, I know this will be very traumatic for you, and I ask you now to be strong for the sake of your wife."

When they arrived at the hospital, they both went directly to the ward.

Mrs Martinez ran to her husband, "Look," she sobbed, "Maria is going to be well! She is breathing fine."

Mr Martinez asked the doctor if they could be alone with Maria.

Both he and his wife sat beside Maria, holding her hand and stroking her hair. After a while, Mr Martinez came into the doctor's office. The doctor could see he had been crying. The poor man could hardly manage to say the words, "Doctor," he stammered, "my wife and I are going to walk to the little church in the hospital grounds. Could you call us when you are ready?"

"Mr Martinez, it's a sad time for everyone, especially you and your wife. I wish there were a better outcome. I will call you as soon as we are ready."

After a little time, the doctor walked slowly down the aisle of the little church almost afraid to disturb them. Both Mr and Mrs Martinez were kneeling at the altar, "Could you please come with me?" the doctor asked softly.

As they entered the ward, there was an eerie silence. No machines and no noise. Only the lifeless body of their young daughter, lying motionless on the bed. The white linen sheets folded neatly under her joined hands, as if in prayer.

The doctor quietly spoke to them, "I will leave you, please stay as long as you wish and, if there is anything you want, please come immediately to my office."

Thank you, doctor," Mr Martinez replied.

About two hours had passed since Mr Martinez and his wife had spoken with the doctor. Mr Martinez took his wife's hand. "It is time now to say goodbye."

Mrs Martinez reached down, kissed her daughter on the forehead and, placing rosary beads in her hands, whispered, "I will never forget you." She turned to her husband and walked towards the door.

Just as Mr Martinez was about to open the door, a faint green glow filled the room, and a moment later, the sound of a feeble voice. "Mama, Mama my head hurts."

Both swung round, incredulously. Maria was lying there motionless, but now her eyes were open, and they could see her chest move with her breathing. She spoke again, "Papa, you came to see me."

Both rushed over to her bedside, tears streaming down their faces.

Maria spoke again, "Why are you crying Mama, is there something bad happening?"

Mrs Martinez put her arms round her daughter. "No my child, nothing bad. Everything is good!"

"Mama, I had a lovely dream." Her mother put her fingers to her daughter's lips. "Not now, you can tell me later."

"Mama, I want to tell you now!" Maria replied. "Emma Sinead and her four friends came to visit me; Emma Sinead told me to go home, it was not my time. What did she mean?"

Her mother answered, "I think it was her way of telling you everything will be fine."

The doctor sat in his office, discussing the case with the staff nurse.

"Doctor," she said, "we will have to move the young girl's body to the mortuary within the next few hours." Before the doctor could answer, Mr Martinez came into the room; he looked different, almost radiant. "Are you all right, Mr Martinez?" asked the doctor.

"Yes, I'm very well, doctor."

"Mr Martinez, I do not want to rush you, but we will have to move Maria soon."

"Doctor," he replied, "you cannot move her now because my wife is talking to her."

"I understand, Mr Martinez. We will leave you there for another hour, then we will have to move her."

"Doctor," said Mr Martinez, "Maria is also talking to her mother."

"Now I don't fully understand you," said the doctor.

"Doctor," replied Mr Martinez. "Maria is awake and talking; she can see us, hear us and talk to us!"

The doctor and nurse rushed out to the ward.

Maria lay there, her eyes open, and talking in a very low voice to her mother.

"Doctor, I told you she would wake up," Mrs Martinez said. "She is badly bruised, but beautiful."

For a moment the doctor was speechless. He began to examine Maria. He lifted her head a little, and placed his hand on the back of her skull: There were no injuries.

"This is unbelievable!" he said, as he turned to the nurse and in a very low whisper, "her skull was crushed and now no injuries: Nothing!"

He spoke to her. "Maria, I am the doctor who treated you when you first came in, and this is the staff nurse; can you see and hear me ok?"

"Yes, doctor," was the feeble reply.

He carefully lifted the covers off her feet. "Maria, I want you to wriggle your toes for me." He held her hand. "Now, move your fingers and squeeze hard on my hand, follow my finger with your eyes."

"I am astounded!" said the doctor.

"Maria," he asked, "do you remember anything about your accident?"

"Nothing, doctor," she replied, "but I do remember my best friend visiting me. She was with four very beautiful ladies; she told me to wake up and go home."

"I see," said the doctor, "and who, may I ask, is your best friend?"

"She is Emma Sinead de Salvador."

The doctor just looked at the nurse and said nothing.

One week later Maria went home, bruised but in good spirits.

Chapter 30

The two coaches made their way from the village of Holy Cross, heading towards Nenagh. Emma Sinead, sitting beside her mother, held her hand and said, "Mama, Maria is going to be ok."

"I hope so," replied her mother, "Maria is a strong girl."

Just then Emma Sinead's phone bleeped. She looked down, one message had arrived. She pressed the message icon, it read, "Thank you, Emma Sinead and your friends, for visiting me. Love Maria xxx."

A big smile came over her face as she handed the phone to her mother, who read the message, then passed the phone to her husband. He turned to Emma Sinead and said, "I have no idea how you did this, and I hope one day I will fully understand everything that is happening." Emma Sinead smiled, "You will Papa."

The two coaches pulled up at the Abbey Field hotel. Peter O'Houlihan spoke with Alex, "I will not be going into the hotel, Alex, I have many jobs to do, so i'll see you all in the morning."

"That's fine," Alex replied, "we will meet tomorrow."

Peter O'Houlihan made his way over to the Salvador family and explained his reasons for leaving immediately and promised to return the next day. He put his arm around Emma Sinead, "You, young lady, are going to be a wonderful Celtic Princess." As he left the coach, he looked down at Michael Hagen who was still sitting in his seat, "Today, Mr Hagen, you have witnessed the power of Celtic Angels."

"You are right Mr O'Houlihan," he replied, "and I hope that one day, I will fully understand what I saw happening today."

"You will, in time, Mr Hagen. In time"

Alex arranged with the hotel to have the use of the private dining room. The manageress, Mrs Mary Clifford, greeted each person individually then guided them through a side entrance, where they slipped in unnoticed.

Once inside the hotel, they could relax and discuss the events of the day. Patrick Ahern introduced his guests to the families and each one in turn talked briefly with the five Princesses.

Emma Sinead sat with the four girls and showed them the text message she had received from her friend Maria. Alessia asked, "Did she see us?"

"Yes," replied Emma Sinead. "Until today, she never knew any of you existed."

"This is great," chuckled Andrea, "no more plane tickets!" everyone laughed.

Saya's mother approached them, "Emma Sinead, we have not had time to sit and talk, shall we go somewhere quiet?"

They both walked to a corner of the room, sat together and talked for a long time.

"Emma Sinead," she said, "you are going to be tall and beautiful, just like the four girls. Listen carefully to all four girls and be guided by them. Over the next few years, you will develop more powers and skills that are unimaginable. Remember, because of you, the girls will become stronger and together, your power will combine, you are most powerful when there are five."

She continued, "Saya has many skills, just like the other girls. I would like Saya to train you in the art of meditation and self-defence, two arts you will need in the future. I will discuss this with your parents."

"Thank you, Mrs Akira," said Emma Sinead, "I look forward very much to learning from Saya."

"I will talk with your parents this evening, and hopefully, in the very near future, Saya will visit you in Buenos Aries."

"I hope so," replied Emma Sinead. "Well, now," Mrs Akira said smiling, "as we have just organised a trip for Saya without her knowing it. Perhaps we should return to the rest of our big family."

Alex stood up, and in his normal loud voice, called for silence, and when he was sure everyone was listening, he continued, "Tomorrow at around noon, we will all be travelling to the Forge, except for Saya and her parents, who have a meeting in the local girls school for ten thirty."

Anabella spoke to Nadia, "As it has been such a long, exciting day, I think we will retire early."

"That seems like an excellent idea Anabella, I will tell Alex," replied Nadia.

The Salvador family left the dining room and made their way to their suite.

When they entered the hotel suite and sat down, Anabella spoke up in a commanding voice, "May I have your attention please, I have something important to say to all of you, including Emma Sinead."

"Not another mystery, Anabella," Jose said, as he laughed. "No mystery," she replied, "just a little surprise."

She sat facing all three, "The house I purchased in Buenos Aries."

"Grandmama," blurted Emma Sinead, "the big house and beautiful gardens that looks like fairyland!"

"Well, Miss Emma Sinead!" Anabella said, smiling, "That big, beautiful house with the fairytale garden is my gift to all of you."

Ellinor looked at Jose in surprise, "I do not understand mother," replied Ellinor, "you are giving us that house?"

"When I first saw the house," Anabella said, "I knew immediately in my heart, that this is where Emma Sinead will grow up. Especially now that she has four new sisters, who will be calling on her from time to time. And you, Ellinor and Jose, have many new friends who will also be visiting."

"But mother, where are you going to live?" asked Ellinor. Anabella replied, "Remember the house by the lake?" Emma Sinead interrupted, "But Grandmama, that's your neighbour's house!"

"I will be your neighbour," replied Anabella, "I purchased both houses.

I do not want to be far away from my lovely grandchild."

"Mother," said Ellinor, "we are speechless! You always think of us."

"Anabella, you are a real angel," said Jose. "Not just yet," replied Anabella, laughing. Jose continued, "I worried about going home with the publicity and the people outside our small house in the city, and wondered how we would all cope?"

"Grandmama, is this true? are we really going to live in the big house?"

"Yes, it's true," she replied, as she hugged Emma Sinead. Looking at Jose and Ellinor, she said, "I arranged, with my government friends, to have everything moved from your house. First to a military facility, and then to your new house. It will give us privacy for a short time on our

151

return to Buenos Aries. We will go directly to the new house, thus avoiding reporters and photographers."

"Mother," said Ellinor, "I don't know what to say. You always think of everything!" Jose replied, "Ellinor, that's the diplomat in your mother, she never lost it," then looking to her husband Ellinor said, "we never imagined that our lives would change so dramatically in such a short time."

"Grandmama," asked Emma Sinead, "can I tell the Princesses we have a big beautiful house with a lake and many trees?"

"You may tell the four Princesses," she replied, "but I am sure they already know!"

Chapter 31

Father Ryan had just completed his weekly round trip of the village of whitethorn. He was content to see everyone happy and cheerful. Mrs McBride's daughter had returned to the village school and settled in as if nothing had happened.

"It must be the spring weather that's making them happy," he thought, as he made his way to his house, next door to the Abbey.

He decided, after a good lunch, he would do some cleaning in the Abbey. With summer fast approaching, as usual, tourists would be arriving with their snapping cameras, photographing anything that moved.

After lunch and a short rest, he made his way along the gravel path towards the Abbey, with his shovel and brush over his shoulder and a large black plastic bag in his hand. He entered the Abbey through the opening where the large doors used to be. He had only walked a short distance when he felt a little strange, muttering to himself as he walked, "I'm sure it's the weather, affecting all of us." He started to sweep the grass and old dead leaves from the Abbey floor, which had blown in the night before, slowly making his way down what was once the centre aisle. As he got closer to the entrance of the underground room, where he had first discovered the broken tablet, he paused for a moment and wondered if he would ever see the five beautiful girls again, or indeed, the broken tablet they had taken with them.

Placing all the dead leaves in the plastic bag, the floor now superficially clean, he looked towards the entrance and muttered, "Now the tourists can come." Leaving his brush and shovel leaning near the entrance of the hidden room, he walked to where the main altar used to be. As he got closer, he noticed a faint green glow, which seemed to come from behind him, casting his shadow onto the wall of the Abbey.

He turned round, facing the entrance. The glow, like an aurora, entered the ruined Abbey through the opening. He walked slowly towards the exit, the light getting brighter. He stopped and stared, squinting his eyes, he could now make out the ghostly figure of a tall girl, wearing a jewelled necklace and a golden tiara which glistened in the light. She moved past him as if he were not there, followed closely behind, by four other girls, each wearing a golden tiara and necklace. The five figures seemed to be floating just above the ground. Their long white dresses disturbing the dust that had remained on the floor. Two of the girls carrying what looked like a stone tablet.

Father Ryan, mesmerised by what he was seeing, stood transfixed. The five figures had brushed past him as if he did not exist, and made their way to the entrance of the underground room. The first figure descended the stone stairs, followed by the other four. He could no longer see them, but felt a deep calmness descending on the whole area, as the green light moved and filled every corner of the abbey. This was something he had never experienced before.

As quickly as it had started, it was over, the green glow that filled the Abbey suddenly disappeared. Father Ryan was rather shaken by what he had seen, in fact, he wondered if it had been his imagination playing tricks on him.

He slowly composed himself and walked towards the entrance of the underground room. Not sure if he was alone, he called out, "Hello!"

There was no reply. He called again, his voice now lower, "Hello?" Again, no reply, just the echo of his voice. He tried peering down, but could see nothing except the last step at the bottom of the stone stairs. He looked around, to make sure there was no one behind him. Nervously, he walked down the stone stairs, one step at a time, until he was standing on the last step. And, just in case he was confronted, he had his shovel in his hand ready to use if necessary. He called again, "Hello?" All was quiet. Not a sound, except for his heart pounding in his chest.

As he reached the bottom of the steps, he turned and walked round to the side. Peering into the room, he was more than surprised to see, leaning upright against the carved Celtic cross, the complete stone tablet. A light, green, glow clearly visible around its edges.

He looked carefully at the tablet. It was complete, and clearly visible were the carved figures of the five Princesses, dressed just as he saw them a few moments ago, and each wearing a jewelled necklace. He murmured to himself as he walked up the stone steps, "They have kept their promise."

Father Ryan thought it best not to tell villagers, until the following day at the Sunday mass, and with a big smile on his face walked slowly back to the church.

Sunday morning, he arose very early and went directly to the ruined Abbey. As he approached the underground room, he wondered if the tablet would still be there, "Maybe it was my imagination?"

He walked carefully down the stone steps and shone his torch into the room. The stone tablet was there, in the same position. Satisfied now, he made his way quickly, back to the church to prepare for his morning service.

He walked with an air of satisfaction along the gravel path leading to the church, some of the villagers were already there. The McBride family had just entered through the main gate.

"Been for your morning walk Father?" asked Mr McBride, he smiled, "just a little stroll to the Abbey," he answered.

Before the service began, the priest stood facing his parishioners and spoke,

"I will be keeping the service short, because today is a very special day for our church and village."

He finished the service quickly and walked up the six steps to the pulpit. He looked down at his dwindling congregation, now no more than thirty-five people. With a smile on his face he said, "The tablet is back and it's complete." There was stunned silence, they waited for him to continue.

"I would like you to follow me." he said, as he walked quickly down from the pulpit, his black robe swishing from side to side, and without changing his pace, he made his way towards the ruined Abbey, the villagers trotting behind trying to keep up with him. On entering the Abbey, the parishioners followed Father Ryan, and one by one walked down the stairs leading to the underground room. As they entered the room, each one stepped forward in turn, touching the tablet and making the sign of the cross.

Someone asked, "Will you bring the tablet into the church Father, like before?"

The priest replied, "The five Princesses placed the tablet in here, and here it must remain until they decide."

"What if someone steals it Father?" another parishioner asked.

"They will protect it," he answered. "Who are we to judge the wisdom of the five Princesses? The tablet will remain here."

Slowly, they made their way out of the room, followed by the priest. On reaching the entrance to the Abbey, they heard a loud rumbling sound and everyone quickly turned round.

"Father!" Mrs McBride said in an excited voice, "the room is covered over again."

"Now it is surely protected!" answered Father Ryan, smiling.

He walked slowly back towards the hidden room, followed by his congregation. They made their way back down the aisle and gazed in amazement. The stone slab, weighing several tons, was indeed in place and covering the hidden room.

"Father!" said Mr McBride, "a few moments ago, that slab was outside, I saw it as I walked in."

They all stood and stared at the stone slab, which had carved in its centre, a large Celtic cross surrounded by the sun, the planets and the seven stars known as the seven sisters or Pleiades. Mrs McBride's daughter called out, "Father! Look, their names are on the bottom of the stone."

Clearly visible were the names of the five Princesses carved deep into the stone, Nikita, Alessia, Andrea, Saya and Emma Sinead.

The priest solemnly spoke, "We must never doubt the wisdom of the five Princesses. They are protecting the tablet, and I am sure, also our village."

Chapter 32

Saya and her parents arrived at the girls school, in the town of Nenagh and went directly to the Head Teacher's office. There they met Kathryn Quirke's form teacher who asked Saya if she and her parents could come into the class quietly and stand at the back.

All four walked down the long corridor towards the classroom, the teacher walked in first, stood in front of her class and called out, "May I have your attention please." At that point, Saya and her parents walked unnoticed into the classroom and stood at the back.

"Children, may I have your attention please," the teacher said, "especially you, Miss Kathryn Quirke." The young Miss Quirke stood up, wondering what she had done.

The teacher said to her, "Kathryn Quirke, a few days ago, you met a Japanese lady in the Abbey Field Hotel, and from what I hear, you said she was crazy."

"No Miss," was the reply, "I just told Saya (that was her name Miss) that my father said she is crazy to climb mountains without safety ropes."

"I also heard you invited her to our school," the teacher said smiling.

"Yes Miss," was the quiet reply.

"Well, Miss Kathryn Quirke, if you would care to look round and see if there is there anyone there you recognise?"

The whole class turned round, Kathryn could not believe her eyes and taken completely by surprise, could only manage a smile.

Saya approached and thanked her for the invitation, by this time the class was buzzing with excitement.

The teacher quickly took control of the situation. She introduced Saya and her parents to the pupils, explaining that Saya could not stay long as it was her last day in Ireland, and she had many things to do.

Saya stood in front of the class and spoke to the children about her life in Tokyo and apologised for the absence of her four friends.

"Miss Saya," one girl said, "my mother said she heard on Tipp FM, there was magic in Holy Cross Abbey yesterday."

"What is Tipp FM?" asked Saya.

"It's our local radio station," replied the teacher. "Well," Saya answered, "I was there with my friends, but I don't know about the magic."

"May I have your autograph, Miss Saya?" the girl asked.

Saya answered, "Well, I cannot just give one of you an autograph, it would not be fair, so I would like you all to take one of your favourite books from your school bag and leave it closed on your desk, and do not open it until I tell you."

With the rustling of school bags, each girl had placed their favourite book on their desk. With a loud tap on the table, the teacher quickly calmed them down.

Saya spent around 45 minutes with the children. She thanked the teacher and all the girls and especially, Kathryn Quirke for the invitation and apologised again for having to leave early. She then walked with her parents towards the door. Kathryn Quirke called, "Excuse me, Miss Saya, what about our books?"

Saya turned, smiled and said, "You may open them now."

The girls opened the books and there were gasps of astonishment. A little green light appeared out of nowhere, and moved quickly over the first page of each book spelling out the words, "Thank you for a lovely time, Princess Saya."

All the girls looked towards Kathryn Quirke and asked, "Is she really a Princess?" and "How did she do that?"

Kathryn just sat there staring at her book, looking at the words, "Thank you, Kathryn for a lovely time, Princess Saya."

For the next few minutes, the teacher had a hard time trying to calm down the excited children. "That was real magic!" she said.

Chapter 33

Alex and Nadia were first into the dining room at the Abbey Field Hotel. Just as they sat at their table, Peter O'Houlihan arrived with his wife.

"Peter," Alex called out, "please come and join us."

As Peter and his wife sat down, he said, "Alex and Nadia, both of you have done a fantastic, wonderful job with the organisation of everything."

"Thank you, Peter," Alex replied, "Now our work begins. We are one family of united parents, with the sole purpose of supporting the five Princesses."

Suddenly, a lot of noise and laughter came from outside the dining room. Alex turned to his wife, "I don't have to say who will appear first, I am sure the whole town of Nenagh will hear them long before they arrive!"

The chatter and laughter coming from the five girls was noticeable, long before they entered the dining room. Four of the girls entered the dining room first, followed by Nikita, and the other parents.

Peter O'Houlihan commented to Ellinor and Jose, "Every time I see the girls, they look more like sisters."

Ellinor was so quick with her answer, which surprised Jose and Anabella, "They are sisters!" she replied.

During breakfast, Peter O'Houlihan handed Anabella a large brown envelope. "A gift, for me?" she asked in a surprised voice. "These are the documents and photographs the parish priest of Carrig promised you."

Anabella opened the envelope, removed the contents and as she looked at her father's photograph, "Look at him," she said, "he was so young. I wonder, did he have any idea, then, what he would achieve in his lifetime and even after he departed?"

Peter replied, "I'm sure, Anabella, your father is looking down on us right now, with that mischievous smile on his face."

"Yes, I think you are right," said Anabella, looking up to the heavens.

Alex tapped on the table and told them, "We will be leaving the hotel for Shannon airport at ten forty-five, our departure is scheduled for Midday. I have made arrangments that we go direct to the plane, security checks will take place at the hanger."

The drive to Shannon was uneventful. The two buses drove direct to the hanger, where the plane was waiting, fully fuelled and ready to leave.

With all the security checks completed, everyone boarded. Nikita and her father appeared from the office carrying the flight plans.

Alex shook the hands of the Irish officials and thanked them for their excellent organisation.

As the Lear jet sped down the runway, Emma Sinead looked at her grandmother and asked, "Did I complete all my tasks the way you wished?"

Anabella just smiled and said, "You completed the mission, just as your great-grandfather would have wished for, we are all so proud of you."

Michael Hagen sat at the back of the plane and talked in-depth to Nadia about the events of the past few days.

The 55 minutes passed quickly and they were soon preparing to land at Gatwick and similarly to their arrival at Shannon, the plane taxied to the private hanger. Customs and immigration officers entered the plane. The chief immigration officer spoke, "Good afternoon, Alex! I hope you had a nice time in Ireland?"

"We had a lovely time," replied Alex.

"And you, Miss Nikita, do you like flying your father's new toy?"

"It's certainly a beautiful plane to fly," she answered.

Customs and immigration checks complete, they drove out of the airport, heading for the Belmont Hotel. Michael Hagen caught the express train to London.

As the coach pulled up outside the Belmont Hotel, Emma Sinead could see the face of Isaac peering through the glass door.

"Mama, Papa look, it's Isaac! He's been waiting for us!"

Her mother replied, "You are going to miss Isaac, when we leave in two days' time for Buenos Aries."

"I know Mama, but I can visit him in my dreams," was the reply.

As they entered the hotel, Isaac, peering out from behind the reception desk, came bounding out to greet them. Going first to Nikita and then to Emma Sinead.

The Salvador family went directly to the lift and the penthouse suite.

Before they entered, Andrea called out, "Emma Sinead, would you like to come jogging with us on the promenade?" Emma Sinead looked at her mother and before the question was asked, her mother replied, "Of course you can."

"Mama, that's magic! I never asked, but you answered."

"Yes, you are right," answered her father, "It's called parent magic!"

After the girls had left, Jose, Anabella and Ellinor sat at a large window, waiting for the five girls to appear on the promenade. The telephone rang, Jose walked over and picked up the phone. "Yes, that will be fine, just come right up."

"Are we having visitors?" asked Ellinor. "Six, to be precise," was the reply. "The parents of Andrea, Alessia and Saya would like to see the penthouse."

They all sat by the large panoramic window overlooking the promenade. "Look!" said Saya's mother, "It's the girls and Isaac."

As they watched the five girls jogging along the promenade, Ellinor said, "We came here with a child and we return to Buenos Aries with a lady."

Andrea's mother spoke up, "From the time Andrea was born, and I know I speak for everyone, our lives have been full of happiness."

"Yes, you are right," said Alessia's mother, "wherever they go, they take happiness with them."

Ellinor called out, "Jose, I think someone is knocking on the door."

Jose walked over and opened it, "Alex, what a surprise! I thought you were resting." Alex walked in and sat down, "Jose, you know very well there's no rest for the wicked!" Everyone laughed. "I have come here for a very special reason. Jose, you and your family will be leaving us in two days' time, all of us here were wondering what little gift could we give you? Something all of you will cherish."

"But first, I have to tell you, eight weeks before you came here to

Brighton, Nikita's dog, Isaac, became a father of ten little babies. Today, the de Salvador family will receive a small gift from Isaac!"

Alex walked over and opened the door, Nadia walked in, with a little pup, now almost 12 weeks old, looking like a mini version of Isaac. She placed him on the floor and immediately, with his tail wagging out of control, he ran from one to another.

Ellinor laughed, "He is so beautiful and so full of life! When Emma Sinead sees him, she will want to keep him."

Alex smiled as he spoke, "As you are moving to a big house with a lake and beautiful gardens, we decided that you needed someone or something (pointing to the pup) to re-design your garden."

Ellinor asked, "What about his travel to Argentina?"

"All the travel arrangements have been made, courtesy of the Argentinean Ambassador," Alex said. "This little dog will be on your plane as you head home. Also, tonight, the Ambassador and his wife will be joining us for dinner."

"Alex," Anabella asked, "the four girls knew about your plan?"

"Yes," he replied, "we needed a plan to get Emma Sinead out of the hotel, and I think they will be making their way back in a few moments."

Alex and Nadia sat down and as they all talked, the son of Isaac amused himself, chasing a fly round the room.

Very soon, the sounds of laughter was heard coming from outside on the corridor. "Quickly," said Alex, "put the dog in Emma Sinead's room."

Soon the door opened, and the five girls entered. As they sat down, Isaac's attention was diverted by a noise coming from the other room, and with his ears almost vertical, he stood up and walked towards Emma Sinead's room. "What's the matter with you, Isaac?" said Emma Sinead, "I am here behind you."

For the first time Isaac paid no attention to her, he scratched at the door and gave a low bark.

"Mama!" said Emma Sinead, "what's wrong with Isaac?"

"Maybe there is someone in your room," she answered. The sound of a short high-pitched bark emanated from inside the room. Isaac could wait no longer, he jumped at the door handle. The door opened and out rushed a little Irish Red Setter, totally ignoring Isaac. Emma Sinead stood there, mouth open wide as if looking for words… "Oh my God, he's gorgeous!"

she said. "Look at him, he's so tiny." She picked him up and as she held him in her arms, she looked to Alex, "What is his name Mr Andrusanke?"

"I'm afraid at this stage he does not have a name, we just call him the son of Isaac."

"Is he really the son of Isaac?" she asked.

"Yes he is," said Alex, "one of ten babies."

Emma Sinead looked over to her mother, "Mama could we steal him and take him back to Argentina?" she asked.

Nikita laughed, "You don't have to steal him Emma Sinead, he is yours and he is going back to Buenos Aries with you."

"Mama, is this true?" Emma Sinead asked, "is he really my dog?"

"Yes, he is your dog," Alex answered, "I have given your father all the legal documents for his travel, but he has to go to the airport tomorrow afternoon to the veterinary department. They will put him on the plane."

"What name will you give him, Emma Sinead?" Alessia asked.

"His name will be Guillermo," she replied.

"Why choose that name?" asked her mother. "Because he is the son of Isaac, and it was William Herschel who expanded Isaac Newton's theory of gravity, and William in Spanish is Guillermo."

Everyone in the room stared in astonishment, amazed by her quick response and the fast choice of name.

"That is a good choice of name," remarked Andrea. The phone rang, Jose answered. He turned to Alex, "The Argentinean Ambassador has arrived."

Alex turned round, "Ok, everyone in the dining room in 30 minutes." As he rushed out of the door. "Mama, what will I do with Guillermo? He cannot stay here alone," Emma Sinead said.

"He can stay in reception with his father," Nikita answered. She then spoke in Russian to Isaac, who barked at Guillermo, and the two walked to the door and waited. Andrea then shouted, "My God, look at the time! We have to be ready in thirty minutes!" Everyone, including Isaac and Guillermo, left the penthouse.

"Emma Sinead," her grandmother said, "quickly to the shower, and put on your green dress for dinner."

When the four girls entered the dining room, Ellinor was happy to see they had dressed in their Celtic dresses.

The dinner went without a hitch, the Ambassador explained to Jose that the Argentine government had organised a special military flight for the family and both he and his wife would accompany them back to Buenos Aries. And the good news for Emma Sinead, her new friend Guillermo would also be on the flight. After long discussions and lots of laughter, the Salvador family made their way back to the penthouse, to prepare for their journey home.

The final day in the Belmont Hotel started with the usual breakfast meeting. Alex welcomed everyone, speaking briefly on the events of the past four weeks, he said, "We will be sad to see the Salvador family leave us today. Four weeks we will never forget. The completion of promises made. Many new friendships forged, but most important, the Fifth Celtic Princess crowned and ready to take her place in a world full of trauma."

Alex then turned to Emma Sinead, "You will face many challenges in your life and with the support from your family, especially your grandmother, you will be strong, wise and fearless. The four Princesses, Nikita, Alessia, Andrea and Saya will always be there to stand by your side when needed. We all wish you Emma Sinead, Dr Jose de Salvador, Mrs Ellinor de Salvador and you, Anabella Fernandez, a safe journey home."

Just as Alex sat down, he stood up again, "I am sorry, I forgot to mention, we will all be visiting you in your new house."

Their bags packed and ready for collection by the hotel porter, the Salvadors' made their way down to reception. "We are all going to the airport with you," said Saya.

Alex and Nadia walked in, "Are we ready?" he asked.

As the coach drove away from the hotel, Emma Sinead asked Saya, "When will you return to Tokyo?"

"My parents and Andreas parents are going to Italy tomorrow, and will stay with Alessia's parents for two weeks and then on their return, I will meet them at Heathrow and fly back to Tokyo." Saya continued, "Remember, Emma Sinead, you only have to think of us. We are always by your side." Each of the girls gave Emma Sinead a hug and a kiss. Emma Sinead, carrying her new friend Guillermo in a small cage, had difficulty holding back the tears as she walked with her parents towards security.

Just before they entered the international lounge, Saya called out, "Do not forget, I will see you in 4 weeks."

Emma Sinead turned, nodded and walked into the VIP lounge, where they were met by the Argentine Ambassador and his wife. Almost immediately, they boarded the waiting military plane for their long flight to Buenos Aries.

Chapter 34

Once on board the military plane, Guillermo soon became the centre of attraction. Emma Sinead sat by her grandmother holding Guillermo tightly in her arms.

As the plane sped down the runway, Emma Sinead felt a little sad, so much had happened in such a short time. Looking out the window as the plane soared higher, she watched the ground become no more than a distant speck. The Belmont Hotel and Brighton were but memories.

The Ambassador explained that there would be a stopover at El Dorado International airport in Colombia, to collect another Ambassador and his young family who were returning to Buenos Aries. With another five hours before they reached El Dorado airport, Emma Sinead asked her mother if she could sleep, and one of the female flight attendants took her to the crew's sleeping area. She climbed into the bunk bed and drew the curtains. She and Guillermo were asleep in minutes.

Later into the flight, Ellinor went back to check, Emma Sinead was fast asleep with Guillermo snuggled up in her arms. Ellinor returned to her husband.

"Is she ok?" he asked, "you should see them, they are going to be the best of friends." Jose walked down and peeked inside the curtain, he returned immediately. "You would not believe it, Guillermo growled at me!"

"He is already protecting her," answered Anabella. Jose laughed, "I hope he learns before he gets much bigger, that I am her father."

"In time he will," said Anabella with a smile.

The landing at El Dorado was on time. The stopover was scheduled to last three hours, giving everyone the opportunity to get out and walk round the shops in the international lounge. The Ambassador and his wife led the way, down the walkway towards the main international lounge, followed by the Salvador family, who had left Guillermo on the plane. As they entered, the Ambassador walked directly to the information desk and enquired about his friends. He was informed that they were not coming to the airport and they had no further information.

As he walked back towards his wife and the Salvador family, there was a loud explosion. The whole building shook, light fittings came crashing down to the floor, the sprinkler system activated, water was gushing out of broken pipes. The blast lifted the Ambassador off the ground and hurled him 30 metres along the floor. A door burst open and four men carrying automatic weapons charged into the lounge, shouting in Spanish, "Everyone on the floor!" brandishing their weapons and firing wildly. Bursts of gunfire echoed throughout the building, followed by a second blast, a huge section of the outer wall came crashing down. The gunmen continued firing in the air.

Anabella crawled along the floor to reach her grandaughter. An elderly man, crouching on the ground beside Emma Sinead, stood up and ran for the door.

There was the loud crack of automatic fire and he collapsed to the ground in a hail of bullets, a large pool of blood emanating from his side and neck.

Jose, without thinking, rushed over to the dying man and placing his hand hard on the side of his neck to stem the flow of blood, he felt the barrel of a gun pressed into the side of his head.

"He is a doctor!" screamed Anabella, as she rushed over. The gunman raised the gun and fired. Anabella fell to the ground, blood streaming from a large wound in her side. Emma Sinead stood up and began to run towards her grandmother, shouting, "Grandmama! Grandmama!"

The second gunman raised his gun and took aim, then realising there was no threat, lowered the weapon. Just as he did Jose shouted out loud, "Emma Sinead get down." She quickly got on all fours and crawled to her grandmother's side. The gunman looked at Jose, raised his foot and kicked him on the side of his head. He slumped over on his back, lying motionless, alongside the seemingly dead passenger.

Emma Sinead cradled her grandmother's head, "Grandmama! please do not leave me, you are going to be ok, please God! Save Grandmama."

In a feeble voice, Anabella answered, "Emma Sinead we need help quickly." Then her last words before she collapsed, "Your necklace! Your necklace!"

One of the gunmen approached, grabbing Emma Sinead by the hair, "Now, I know you!" he shouted. "You're the smart little girl who met the Queen of England. Well, she will not help you now!" Then shouted to one of his fellow terrorists, "Look at the prize we have here!" as he dragged Emma Sinead across the floor.

Grabbing his arm with both hands, trying to make him release his grip, she remembered her grandmother's words. She released her grip on his arm, and placed her hand on her chest, to the now invisible necklace, she uttered a faint cry, "Please help us."

Almost immediately, the whole departure hall was illuminated by a green glow. Emma Sinead looked at the gunman and in a strong voice said, "I am not your prize!"

Taken aback by her protest, he bellowed at her, "You little rich bitch," and raised his gun to strike her. Suddenly, a hand grabbed him from behind, he went flying across the room without his gun. The voice he heard was that of Andrea, "Get your filthy hands off my sister!" Another of the gunmen raised his gun and fired a quick burst from his automatic. Andrea continued to walk towards him. The bullets passed right through her, but she continued towards him. Now completely confused, he raised his gun to fire again. Too late! Andrea grabbed him by the neck and with her other hand, took his gun and smashed it to pieces. Then, picking him up like a rag doll, she threw him across the room, knocking over the third gunman who was standing there in shock at what he had just witnessed.

Alessia sat with Ellinor and the ambassador's wife, protecting and comforting both, the Ambassador's wife now screaming and crying aloud for her husband, who lay on the floor more than 30 metres from them.

Ellinor spoke, "Alessia, go and help Andrea." Alessia smiled, "She is doing very well on her own, Mrs de Salvador."

Saya turned towards the fourth gunman and without uttering a word, he lowered his weapon slowly to the ground. She reached out and placed her hand on his forehead, he collapsed to the ground.

Emma Sinead looked towards Saya, and without a word being spoken, she placed her hand on the gaping wound in her grandmother's side. A green glow surrounded them both. After a few moments, the bleeding stopped and the wound disappeared. Her grandmother opened her eyes and spoke softly, "Is it over?"

"Yes, Grandmama, it's over. The girls are here to protect us." Anabella sat up and looked around, "Emma Sinead! quickly, go to your father, he needs you!"

Emma Sinead rushed to her father's side, holding his hand gently, and as a green glow enveloped him, she called to him, "Papa, please wake up."

Jose opened his eyes and with a confused voice asked, "Emma Sinead, are you ok?"

"I am fine Papa, it's over." Jose sat up, still a little dazed. He leant over to the elderly man lying on the ground, "There is nothing I can do for this poor man," he said. "Papa, we will look after him, now you go to Mama."

Saya, kneeling beside the Ambassador, placed her hand on his forehead. Speaking in a calm voice, she said, "Mr Ambassador, can you hear me?"

The Ambassador opened his eyes, "What happened? Saya, how did you get here?" Saya answered, "There is no time to explain. You must leave this place immediately."

Nikita had already taken care of the last two terrorists, who were now sitting against the remains of the outer wall, as if sleeping. Passengers and friends walking dazed through the smoke-filled building. "We must leave now," Nikita said, "it's over." They could hear the sound of sirens in the distance, as Saya and Nikita walked through the rubble of the international lounge. Nikita took charge, saying, "Quickly! Saya get everyone we must go." Alessia placed her hand on the forehead of the Ambassador's wife, and in a moment, she was sitting peacefully on the ground staring blankly into space.

"She will recover later, and remember nothing of this," Alessia said.

The four girls then went to where the body of the first victim lay. Emma Sinead sat beside him, holding his hand and as they placed their hands on his chest, a green glow enveloped all five Princesses. Slowly, he started to breath, then, placing him in a sitting position by the wall, Nikita spoke, "He will be ok and not remember anything. Emma Sinead, is your father all right?"

"Yes, he is fine, just dazed.," was the reply.

The four girls walked quickly, guiding the Salvador family and the Ambassador, who was now supporting his wife, through a smoke-filled side entrance. They ran along the walkway towards the plane. Jose was the last to enter, he turned to talk with Nikita, but the girls were gone.

The crew ushered them quickly to their seats, shouting out loudly, "quickly! we have to leave here immediately!" They clambered in and sat on the nearest seats available. The pilot had already notified the tower that they were ready to go, the door was quickly closed, and the four engines roared into life.

As the plane was careering down the runway, Emma Sinead staring out the window, could now clearly see the large gaping hole on the side of the international lounge and the flashing blue lights of many police cars. The Ambassador's wife, still in shock, sat with two flight attendants. Anabella turned to the Ambassador and spoke very quietly, "Mr Ambassador, what you have seen here today, you cannot mention to anyone. We were not in the lounge."

"Yes, I think I understand," he replied. "Anabella, where did the girls come from?"

Anabella just put her finger to her lips.

The plane, now at cruising altitude, the captain came back to see them. "Are you all ok?" he asked.

The Ambassador replied, "Just a little shaken and dusty." "You were all fortunate not to have reached the international lounge," the captain said, "I believe a bomb destroyed it."

"Very lucky indeed!" said the Ambassador, as he turned to his wife. "Are you ok my dear?" "I am fine," she replied, "I must have hit my head and fallen, I cannot remember what happened."

Anabella smiled and made no comment.

The flight soon settled down. Emma Sinead sitting with her grandmother and Guillermo.

Her grandmother spoke in a soft voice, "Today, you have seen the power of your necklace. The Angels were watching us and could have intervened, but you needed to learn the power of the necklace." Which was now clearly visible round Emma Sinead's neck. As Anabella continued, she lowered her voice, "Your ability to control the power of the necklace will improve as you get older, and allow you to do much more. The angels and your great-grandfather will always be there, watching over you."

Emma Sinead answered, "Grandmama, I was so scared! I could not think, but now, I know the angels are always watching over me, and in the

170

future, I will be more aware."

"There is much to learn," her grandmother replied, "and that is why Saya is coming to teach you."

Emma Sinead then went over and sat beside her father and mother. Ellinor still shaking a little from the ordeal.

Emma Sinead held her mother's hand, "Mama, it's ok, we are safe now."

Ellinor squeezed her hand, "You were so brave," she said as she cried, "the way you rushed to your father's side, I was so sure they would kill you."

Emma Sinead answered as she hugged her mother, "You mama, papa and Grandmama are my family, and no one can come between us. Only the one God can separate us."

For the next hour, Emma Sinead walked Guillermo up and down the plane to tire him out. Anabella suggested, "I will hold him for a while, you go and sit with your mama and papa," and within minutes, Guillermo was fast asleep in her arms.

Emma Sinead laughed, "Grandmama, you are a baby Guillermo sitter."

"Well," her grandmother replied, "I hope baby Guillermo does not make a habit of this, especially when he gets older and bigger like his father!" she laughed.

Emma Sinead, now sitting with her mother and father, "Mama, papa," she said, "Saya will be with us soon?"

Ellinor replied, "It will just give us enough time to organise our new house. Can you ask Saya to let us know the flight she will be on, we can collect her at the airport." Emma Sinead looked at her mother and smiled.

The military plane landed at the air force base just outside Buenos Aries. Emma Sinead turned to her mother, "Mama it was nice to go to England, but it is lovely to come home, especially to our new house, I think Guillermo is going to like it."

They spent a short time at the airbase talking with the commander, he told them, "You were all lucky not to have reached the international lounge." And then spoke with the ambassador. The commander explained the Colombian security forces had failed to inform the flight of a possible terrorist threat. However, they had informed the Argentine Ambassador to Colombia, who had changed his plans. "I have been instructed by our president to hold a full enquiry into the event." Turning again to Jose,

"Doctor I can only apologize to you and your family for the situation you got caught up in, and over the next coming weeks if you don't mind we will talk again. In the meantime, I am sure you are all very tired and have homes to go to."

The Salvador family left the military base, and were driven to their new home by the military police. Around one hour later, they arrived at the entrance of the property. Ellinor asked, "Why are the police here?" The driver answered, "As far as I am aware m'am, it is a temporary measure for a few months, to discourage the Press."

There were now two very large cast iron gates, which the driver opened by pressing a remote control in the car. "These are new," said Anabella.

"Wow! this is cool," remarked Emma Sinead. The car drove down the long, tree lined drive, "It looks just like England," remarked Emma Sinead.

Anabella entered the house first, expecting to be greeted by a mountain of boxes, but to her surprise, there was not a box in sight. "They have unpacked everything," she said.

Ellinor suggested Anabella stay with them for a few days, before moving to her house by the lake. "I thought you would never ask!" replied Anabella.

"Grandmama," said Emma Sinead, "you can stay here forever, if you like, we have lots of room."

"Thank you, Emma Sinead, for the kind offer, but remember I have my life to live and my circle of friends. Anyway, I am only a five-minute walk from the main house."

During the next two weeks, several government officials came to the house to discuss the terrorist attack and Emma Sinead's meeting with the British Royal family, also to inform the family of the progress the two governments were making regarding the islands.

Emma Sinead appeared on many TV channels and spoke with several journalists. Her photograph continued to appear in the newspapers. She returned to her school, and after a short time, the excitement of the school children faded away and life returned to normal.

A few weeks later, on returning from school, Emma Sinead asked her mother if her friend Maria could stay on Saturday night.

"Of course she can, we would love to see her," was the reply. "Do we have to collect her?"

Emma Sinead replied, "Her parents will bring her over on Saturday morning, if that is ok."

"That's fine," said her mother. "I will tell the police at the gate. Also, do you think you should tell Guillermo?"

"He already knows," was the reply, "I told him yesterday."

Later, as they were preparing dinner, Ellinor spoke, "Emma Sinead, it's four weeks and we have not heard from Saya. Maybe she forgot."

Emma Sinead looked at her mother, "She has not forgotten mother, she will arrive."

As the Salvador family sat round the table for their evening meal, the front door bell rang twice. "Jose," said Ellinor, "I think we have a visitor."

"The police normally ring when we have visitors," he replied. Jose walked towards the door and opened it slowly.

"Saya!" he said, "we were just talking about you, come in, please, come in."

Jose walked with Saya to the dining room. "Look who has arrived!"

Emma Sinead stood up and gave Saya a hug, "I knew you would be on time."

Jose spoke, "Saya, you should have telephoned when you arrived at the airport. I could have collected you."

Saya looked at Jose and smiled, "I did not come by plane."

"How did you persuade the police to let you in the main gate?" Jose asked.

"Oh," Saya said smiling, "they never noticed me as I passed by."

Jose laughed, "Ok, I am not even going to ask how you do it."

"Tomorrow, I will have to introduce you to the police at the main gate, otherwise they will treat you like a criminal."

Anabella said warmly, "Saya, it is so good to see you!" Ellinor pulled a chair away from the table, "Please Saya, sit here." They laughed and talked well into the night.

Emma Sinead spoke, "Saya, my friend Maria is coming here tomorrow, is it ok with you if she stays here the night?"

"Of course, I would love to meet her again."

Saya's answer surprised Jose, but he chose to ignore it and asked, "How are your parents?"

"They are all fine," replied Saya. "They went back to Tokyo last week." She continued, "Andrea said to tell you, they may visit us in a week or two."

"Well," answered Jose, "that will liven up the place!"

The next morning, Maria arrived with her parents. As they all sat talking in the lounge, Saya walked in. Maria, lost for words, just stared. She turned to her mother and in a whisper said, "That's Saya, who was in my dream at the hospital."

Maria's mother stood up and embraced Saya, "I have no words to thank you."

"It was our pleasure," answered Saya.

Maria said, "I saw you in my dream, Miss Saya."

"Well," replied Saya, "it must have been a good dream."

"It was the best!" responded Maria.

The weekend went by quickly. Anabella suggested Emma Sinead and Saya should stay in her house, there, Saya could begin to teach Emma Sinead, and of course, Guillermo. This became the usual routine for the next few weeks, resulting in Emma Sinead gaining more power and confidence every day.

On Tuesday, two weeks later, Doctor Jose came home early. He suggested they would all go into the city of Buenos Aries shopping, and later dine at a nice restaurant. "That's a lovely idea," answered Ellinor.

"Where are the two girls?" he asked. "Emma Sinead and Saya are in the woods with Guillermo. I think they are teaching him how to hunt."

They were interrupted by a commotion outside. Jose looked out the window, "Oh my God, they have arrived!"

Ellinor called out from the kitchen, "What's happening, who has arrived?" "The girls, can you not hear Andrea laughing?"

All five girls stormed into the house, "Mama, papa, look who has arrived!" shouted Emma Sinead.

A few days later, the five Princesses went with Anabella to her house. "Grandmama," Emma Sinead said, "we are taking you on a journey to complete the task."

"But it's hundreds of kilometers away in Patagonia!" replied Anabella.

Emma Sinead replied softly, "Grandmama, you will be safe with us."

The five Princesses stood in a circle around Anabella. Emma Sinead spoke, "Grandmama, close your eyes."

As fast as she closed and opened her eyes, they were there, standing on a hill overlooking the farm. Emma Sinead took out the small box and placed it in Anabella's hand and solemnly said, "It is for you, Grandmama, to complete the task." Anabella stooped down, and carefully sprinkled the contents on the grave. Immediately, the sky above turned different shades of green lights.

"It is complete, Grandmama, look up at the sky. All the Celts are dancing!"

Anabella stood and stared, "It's so beautiful! How could I explain something like this to anyone?"

Nikita spoke, "Anabella, it's time to return." They stood round her and told her to close her eyes, the return journey home was every bit as fast as the journey out.

Next morning on television, there were reports of strange green lights over south Patagonia. The newscaster said it was a powerful Aurora Australis, never before seen in daylight.

Jose just smiled, looked at the five Princesses and said, "I wonder who was responsible for that."

Chapter 35

Isaac Going Home

Isaac, by now was getting old, his health failing and with little time left. Nikita had asked the angels for permission to interfere in the natural cycle of life, it was agreed. The five Princesses would take Isaac to Whitethorn Abbey, on the evening of Christmas eve. There, the angels would come and take him home, to the third planet of the largest star in the Pleiades.

Father Ryan had worked hard, in the ruins of the old abbey preparing for a special Christmas Eve service, to honour the five Princesses. He had decorated the walls inside with colourful lights. The villagers had helped him erect an altar on the stone slab covering the hidden room, and there they placed a large, stone Celtic cross they had manhandled in from the grounds surrounding the abbey, this was to be the centrepiece. Father Ryan suggested to his congregation, as the Abbey had no roof or doors, to dress in warm clothing, and with God's help the weather would remain fine.

At 21:00 hrs on Christmas Eve, the service began, each parishioner holding a lighted candle. Father Ryan stood beside the new altar, and just as he was about to begin his sermon, a gentle warm breeze began to blow through the entrance. The temperature rose as the breeze sent the last of the autumn leaves dancing down the aisle. All the candles flames now fluttering in the breeze gave the abbey an enchanted feel. The priest and congregation turned and looked towards the entrance. Suddenly, the Abbey was bathed in a soft green glow and the ghostly figures of the five Princesses appeared through the entrance. They seemed to be drifting with the wind as they moved slowly down the aisle, the leading figure holding, on a leash, a frail Irish red setter by her side. As they reached the newly built altar, they turned and stood in front of the Celtic cross and transformed into the five Princesses.

Nikita spoke to the priest and congregation, "Father and the people of

Whitethorn, we came here this night to save the life of our very special friend. His name is Isaac, he has been our faithful friend for many years and we will not abandon him, his life now almost at an end, we must act fast. Soon the angels will come for him and take him to a place you call heaven, but we call home, there he will be loved and live forever, awaiting our reunion."

Emma Sinead then spoke, "Please, do not be scared of what will soon take place, there is nothing to be afraid of." Isaac lay down in front of the Celtic cross, a feeble movement of his tail was the only sign of life in his weakening body. The five Princesses stood by his side facing the entrance to the abbey. The priest and his parishioners sat in awestruck silence.

From high above the abbey, two small green lights appeared like falling stars, descending to the ground and hovering for a moment near the five princesses, before evolving into two tall girls each wearing a long, white, Celtic dress and necklace, similar to the ones the five Princesses wore. Both wore golden tiaras which glistened in many colours from the lights on the walls of the Abbey. As they approached the altar, the five Princesses moved to one side and bowed to the approaching figures, who walked slowly towards Isaac. They placed their hands gently on him, and as if floating on air, his frail body rose from the ground and with the two figures by his side, they moved slowly down the centre aisle towards the exit. The priest and small congregation, mesmerised by the event they were witnessing, looked on in silence. The daughter of Mr and Mrs McBride looked up, then nudging her mother she said in an excited voice, "Mother look at the sky." Immediately everyone looked up, the abbey and the sky above was alive with dancing coloured lights. Before the ghostly figures had reached the exit, the lights became brighter, and in a flash, they were gone.

The five Princesses turned to face the priest and his parishioners. Andrea spoke, "Our dear friend, Isaac, has gone to our home, one day in the distant future, we will unite with him. We wish you all peace and happiness at this time." The five Princesses then walked slowly towards the congregation, and held the hand of each person in turn. As Emma Sinead approached the McBride family, she reached out and held the hand of their daughter. She spoke softly, "Your destiny is assured. In the distant future you will become a great leader."

Returning to the altar, they bowed to the Celtic Cross, then, facing the congregation, held hands and the five Princesses disappeared into the night sky. A few moments later, large snowflakes began falling gently on the congregation.

Father Ryan looked up at the falling snowflakes and spoke to his congregation, "The five Princesses chose our Abbey to help an ailing friend and show us the true meaning of Christmas. Let us say a prayer of thanks to them for reminding us, that not only is Christmas a time for love and peace, but every day should be so."

A few days after Christmas, local papers and television reported that a beautiful Aurora Borealis was visible to many people over the Western Isles of Scotland on the evening of Christmas Eve.

Finally

Over the next few years, Emma Sinead, guided by her family and the four Princesses, completed her schooling and is preparing to enter University, studying astro and space engineering.

The Malvinas Islands, now under the joint management of the United Kingdom and Argentina. A large photograph of Emma Sinead presenting a bunch of flowers to Queen Elizabeth hangs on the wall of Port Stanley Airport with the heading, "We built a bridge."

Guillermo, (son of Isaac) has matured and inherited his father's ways. Now a fully grown Irish red setter, he spends his day alternating between Anabella and Ellinor's home, trying to do what all Irish red setters do best, modifying the gardens.

Trouble on the horizon in

Book Two

The Fifth Princess and the Black Pearl

Printed in Great Britain
by Amazon